Adam Nicke was born near Caerleon in Wales on the Lupercalia, just a few miles from where the Gothic author Arthur Machen was born in 1863.

In his early twenties his artistic tendencies were expressed in the designing and making of clothes, most notably for Wayne Hussey of The Mission.

In his previous novel, Temptation and Denial, he railed against the hypocrisy and misogyny of those that use religion as a tool of control; in this satirical novel his recalcitrant disposition finds fertile ground in attacking today's political ruling elite by placing their ignorance, superstition, and self-serving dishonesty in 18th century Wales. He has a degree in Literary Studies from the University of the West of England.

Adam Nicke Publishing

Reviews left on Amazon or Goodreads help promote the books you love.

Published by Adam Nicke Publishing, 2020
adamnicke@gmail.com

Cover design by Adam Nicke
Imprint: Independently published

ISBN: 9798634456492 (Paperback)

Mallard the Quack

Adam Nicke

Adam Nicke was born near Caerleon in Wales on the Lupercalia, just a few miles from where the Gothic author Arthur Machen was born in 1863.

In his early twenties his artistic tendencies were expressed in the designing and making of clothes, most notably for Wayne Hussey of The Mission.

In his previous novel, Temptation and Denial, he railed against the hypocrisy and misogyny of those that use religion as a tool of control; in this satirical novel his recalcitrant disposition finds fertile ground in attacking today's political ruling elite by placing their ignorance, superstition, and self-serving dishonesty in 18th century Wales. He has a degree in Literary Studies from the University of the West of England.

Adam Nicke Publishing

Contents

Do You Like My Muff, George?

"It's like this Doctor," the red-faced farmer began. Casting his eyes around the room as though he were about to betray a confidence and wanted to be doubly sure no one was eavesdropping, he drew himself forward on his seat and lowered his voice. "I'm having trouble with my *little ploughman*. I just can't get him to rise in the morning like I once could," he whispered. With that, he let out a deep sigh and slumped backwards in his chair, as though a heavy burden had been lifted from his shoulders.

"I see," replied Doctor Ivor Mallard, Surgeon, Barber and Apothecary. He, of course, was no Doctor. He had started life as a travelling quack, wandering from place to place selling his 'patented' remedies. After begging, borrowing, and stealing enough money, he had bought into a permanent practice with his long-time employer and partner-in-crime Doctor Ronald Stumpf, a charlatan of the highest rank and a firm believer in the notion that sparing the rod spoiled the child. The fact that this personal philosophy didn't adhere to just children and took in any form of malingerer, be they sick or healthy, was immaterial as all most people needed was a 'good horsewhipping'.

Over the years, both Doctors had sold their pills and potions at fayres before quickly moving on before the locals realised that *Doc Mallard's Laxative Deodorant* or *Doctor Ronald Stumpf's Holy Spirit Tanning Lotion* were not the products they'd been promised. Still, given Stumpf paid the wages, Mallard agreed the shade of orange Stumpf had turned was irrefutable evidence that the Holy Spirit was flowing through the flabby old huckster.

"Well, it's a common enough problem in men of your age," Mallard said. "Many men find they have trouble with their *little ploughman* once in a while. If you'd like to pop behind the screen and drop your britches, I'll have a look at the little fella."

"Uh, right you are Doctor," replied the farmer, looking a little nervous and beginning to frown. Nonetheless, he rose from his seat. "Are you sure this is going to help?"

"Trust me ... I *am* a Doctor," Mallard replied, puffing up his chest and reclining in his seat, before folding his arms.

Slowly, the farmer moved to the screen and with a little reluctance, dropped his britches. Finally, naked from the waist down, his bright red buttocks quivering like apples bobbing in a barrel of water, he stood as still as he could whilst clutching his britches in front of him.

"All done, Doctor," he said, his voice cracking.

"Good, good. Now if you could just let me have a look at him," Mallard commanded, in his best Doctorly tones.

With great reluctance, the farmer moved, stepped away from the screen and walked toward the Doctor.

"Now let me see," Mallard began, moving from his side of the desk. Sitting in a chair in front of the farmer, so that his head was level with the man's groin. "Well, I can't see anything wrong. How long have you noticed there to be a problem?" asked Mallard, as he peered intently over the top of his spectacles.

"I'm not sure. I think it was when I docked his wages for coming into work drunk a few months back," the farmer replied.

Mallard unleashed his grip on the appendage so quickly one could be forgiven for thinking hot embers had been dropped into his hand.

"When you said *little ploughman*, you meant ..."

"Little ploughman. Look, there he is," said farmer, pointing through the window at a small dishevelled-looking labourer on the far side of the road. As Mallard moved to the window and peered through the glass, the man spied the learned Doctor's attention and gave a little wave.

"Oh, so that's your little game, is it?" Ivor shouted, turning sharply on the farmer, who took a step backwards in surprise before losing his footing in the britches around his ankles and falling to the ground.

"Eh?" said the farmer, wrestling with his tangled apparel.

"Don't think I don't know what you farmers are like! Oh yes! *Let's go and see old Mallard. He's always good for a cheap fondle*! Well not me, my friend! I bet you've been scheming over this one for months, haven't you? You disgust me! Here I am, a qualified and caring Doctor having to put up with the likes of you! There are sick people in need of my attention and all you can think about is how you're going to get your next sordid thrill! My God, what do you take me for? Now get out of here before I stick my boot in your little ploughman's lunchbox!"

"No Doctor, it really is my little ploughman," the farmer protested.

"Unbelievable! Just because I'm devilishly handsome, *everyone* thinks they're in with a chance!" Ivor said incredulously. "I may have strong, firm Doctor's fingers but ..." before trailing off and taking the farmer by the scruff of the neck, dragging him face down to the door.

"No, Doctor, you don't understand," the farmer protested, wincing as a splintered floorboard caught him in a sensitive area.

Ivor threw the half-dressed farmer into the waiting room and brushed his hands.

"And next time you want a cheap thrill then see Doctor Stumpf!"

Meanwhile, in the consulting room next door Doctor Stumpf was busy.

"So you see, in the Gospel according to … uh … Neville in the Bible it states *And lo, God saw that Beelzebub had been so jealous of Doctor Stumpf's really beautiful feet he had accursed him with bone spurs and so God had a word with the Holy Spirit and they sent Doctor Stumpf some ointment and his feet were tremendous again,*" Doctor Stumpf explained.

"I see," said the patient. "Have you studied the Bible, then?" the patient asked.

"*Nobody* reads the Bible more than me!" Stumpf replied.

"Yes, I can see that hermeneutics is your thing," the patient said, causing Stumpf to shift uneasily in his seat.

"Herman who?" he replied, loosening his collar.

"Hermeneutics!"

"*Nobody* reads Herman's ethics more than me! Tremendous book … a really great guy," Stumpf replied.

"Was there anything else, Mrs Jones?" Mallard asked, unaware of what was unfolding in the surgery next door. Suddenly, a scream rang out from Stumpf's consulting room. "What the fu ... flip was that?" Ivor exclaimed, jumping from his chair so quickly that by the time it had fallen to the floor he had already reached his surgery door. Already he had swung it open and was halfway to Doctor Stumpf's surgery in the adjacent room.

"I was only teasing! I know you know more about hermeneutics than anyone and knew you knew it was the study of the Bible!" cried a terrified voice from far inside the room.

Quickly, Ivor opened the door. There, before him, a young man ran terrified around the small surgery, trying his best to avoid Doctor Stumpf as the flabby old charlatan snorted and sweated behind him.

"What's going on?" Ivor asked as Stumpf slumped back into his chair.

"He's crazy! He told me that there's a passage in the Bible that says his foot ointment was sent by God! Then he said I had 'softening of the brain' and that he needed to knock a hole in my head with his golf club to let out the vapours!"

10

"It will be really great ... tremendous! One hole in the skull and all my - uh, *your* - problems will be over!" Stumpf slurred.

With that, the patient fled.

"What was it this time, Doctor Stumpf?" Ivor inquired.

"A know-all ... far too cocky. He also looked a bit foreign," Stumpf replied, still snorting and wheezing.

"Nurse Conwy, could you please get Doctor Stumpf a pot of tea? He's not looking himself."

"Thank God for that!" muttered Nurse Conwy as she approached the open surgery door.

"What did you say?" Mallard asked, still blindly loyal to him that paid the wages.

"Oh ... uh ... God forbid," said the nurse, narrowing her eyes and looking at Mallard as Mallard narrowed his eyes and returned her gaze.

"Hmm, okay," Ivor said suspiciously as the woman left.

"How much do we pay Nurse Conwy?" asked Stumpf.

"As little as possible. Why do you ask?" Ivor replied.

"Because she's wearing gold jewellery. Where does she get the money?" he asked. Before Ivor had a chance to respond, the two Doctors were interrupted by a quiet voice from near the door.

"I'll just be off then, Doctor."

"I'm sorry, Mrs Jones. Yes, yes of course," Ivor said, taking the woman by her arm and leading her to the front door. "And tell that husband of yours he's a lucky man," he added, thinking himself quite a charmer.

Returning to Ronald's surgery, Ivor braced himself. He had news for Ronald and had been delaying telling him. 'Strike whilst the iron is hot', Ivor thought to himself.

"Doctor Stumpf - Sir - sit down, please. I have some important news for you ... well, for *us*. I had a letter from my father today. He wrote that George - my half-brother George, remember? He's finished his studies in Edinburgh. Well, he was told to leave on account of his being a moron! Anyway, he wants to come back here and pick up some practical knowledge from a couple of old pros like us. Bloody college boys! There will be more than a few shillings in it for you ...."

"Yes. He's a really great guy ... unbelievable!" came the prompt reply, interrupting Ivor's best sales patter.

"Yes? You don't want to look at his testimonials?"

"No, I certainly do not!" Ronald replied emphatically, evidently misunderstanding what was meant by the word 'testimonials'.

"Good! Then I've no reason to send word for him not to come. He'll be here on ..." Ivor said, drawing the letter from his pocket to check the date. "The fifth, which is ... tomorrow! Oh bollocks, I didn't realise he'd be here so soon."

Ronald said nothing as he took another swig of liniment rub and closed his eyes.

The rest of the day passed quietly, with Ivor making a few home remedies and Ronald 'relaxing'.

At around nine the following morning, a loud banging rang through the entire house as the knob of a cane rapped at the old back door.

"Oh, God, another day," Ivor mumbled as the noise woke him. "Can someone answer the door?" he shouted. There was no reply.

Slowly, he climbed from his bed and made his way through the house towards the back door, stopping just before he got to it to open a door to his left.

"Nurse Conwy, someone is knocking the door. Nurse Conwy, would you open the door and let whoever's knocking it in, please?" Ivor hissed, before turning and going back to bed.

Nurse Conwy roused herself and moved towards the commotion.

"Alright! Alright! Who's banging away at this time in the morning?" she shouted, as she pulled back the bolts and swung open the door. There, she was greeted by the scrubbed and shining face of young George Uppham, half-brother to Ivor Mallard and heir to the entire Uppham estate that Mallard found himself denied, on account of his being a swine.

"Morning! Remember me? I think I'm expected. George Uppham." said George, extending his hand and taking Nurse Conwy's hand in his. He was about to kiss it until he noticed how dirty it was and thought better of it.

"Expected? I should say! You can bang away at my door any time," Nurse Conwy said, doing her best to look beguiling as she gave a smile that showed more gaps than teeth.

"May I come in?" George asked.

"Ooh, you saucy devil! I can see I'm going to have to watch you!" Nurse Conwy replied, playing with her hair.

"No, I meant ..." George felt himself redden. "May I enter?"

"Ooh, you'll be getting me into trouble!" said Nurse Conwy, giving George a push on the shoulder in mock indignation.

At the risk of saying anything further, George moved past the woman and dropped his sack and suitcase on the floor.

"I expect you're all hot and sweaty after such a long journey, what with such a full sack! I bet you can't wait to unload it," Nurse Conwy said, spying what George had just dropped.

"No, I'm fine, honestly," George answered, as Nurse Conwy drew nearer.

"Go on! I bet you're hot and sticky all over," she continued.

"Is that George?" Ronald shouted, having heard an unfamiliar voice echo up the stairs. "I'll show you your room. Thank you, Nurse Conwy, that'll be all," Ronald said, making a motion to pick up George's things before having second thoughts and casting Nurse Conwy a withering look. "You'll have to learn to ignore Nurse Conwy," he continued, as Nurse Conwy returned to her room and slammed the door. "She's like that. I remember the time my dear friend Peregrine visited before he was thrown out of his military academy and joined a travelling ballet company in Greece. He used to weep every time she spoke to him," he added, before pausing and gazing wistfully into the distance.

15

"It's looking stormy out there," George said, making small talk with the old mountebank.

"What was that? I was miles away. You were saying there may be a storm tonight?"

"Yes, stormy."

"Don't say such things! I've got an aversion to *anything* stormy!" Ronald said, his face drawn into a scowl.

"Right you are," George replied, looking a little askance at Doctor Stumpf for the abrupt change of conversation.

"I'll show you your room and leave you to settle in," Ronald said. "It must be a real pleasure for you being here with me, George. By the way, you didn't forget the cheques for Doctor Mallard and me, did you?"

George patted his breast pocket and smiled, as Stumpf drew alongside George's room and entered.

"Oh damn! I wanted to have a word with the driver of your carriage before he left. Is he still there?" Stumpf asked as George moved to the window.

"He's just pulling off!" George replied.

"The filthy swine!" said Stumpf.

"Uh? Oh wait, he's finished! Now it looks like he's getting ready to leave," George said, as the crunch of wheels on cobblestones echoed up from the road.

"Hmm," Stumpf said, drawing out the word and giving George a long look as he closed the door and left.

Storm clouds were gathering and very soon, deep rumblings came over the black hills and the gentle tapping of rain on the tiles of the town. George began to unpack his things, hoping very much for a flash of lightning. Then, all of a sudden, a quick succession of bolts darted across the sky.

Quickly, George undressed. After uncoiling a length of flex and attaching one end to a length of copper, he opened the window and clambered out onto the roof.

Ivor lit his pipe and took a swig of laudanum. With no patients today, this was his time to relax. Suddenly, there was the sound of heavy footsteps outside his door, then the handle was turned and the door kicked open.

"Have you looked out of the window?" Ronald demanded, his face dark orange with rage.

"Since we lived here, or just recently?" asked Ivor, the laudanum having already worked its wonders.

"There's a naked man just run past my window with a length of metal in his hands," Ronald shouted, becoming increasingly agitated at Ivor's lack of concern.

"Ronald, I want you to answer me truthfully - have you been drinking the liniment rub again?" Ivor asked, trying his best to sound as rational as possible.

"No! It's that halfwit brother of yours! Is it some custom around your part of the world to show everything you've got when reacquainting yourself in a district or something?" Ronald raged, not rising to Ivor's flippant retort.

"What!" Ivor said, with sudden alarm, before rushing to the window. "George, don't do it!" he shouted. Upon hearing his name, George turned but in so doing slid on the slippery wet tiles and plummeted earthwards. "Ah, well, got him off the roof, anyway," he added, turning back towards the door with a smile on his face

Ivor carried George indoors and let him rest until the following morning when he was awoken by Ivor and given a list of patients that had made appointments for the day.

"Right George, here are the suckers you have to see today. Come on, shake a leg," Ivor said, pulling the sheets off George and poking him in the ribs.

"Yes. Sorry, Ivor. What's the time?" George said, reaching out a hand to his pocket watch on the bedside table. "Half-past eight," he mumbled to himself, shaking the sleep from his eyes and propping himself up against the headboard. Finally, he was ready to listen to what Ivor had to say about his duties for the day.

"Right, at half-past nine you have David Jones. He's had a break-up and is after something to ease his mind. At ten, you've got David Jones and he's got a problem with his feet. At half-past-ten, you have David Jones who has something horrible he's picked up at sea for us to look at. At eleven you have David Jones and he has some shot in his arse where one of the locals shot him. Last thing this morning - at half-past-eleven - you have David Jones. He fell down the stairs after taking off his belt to belt some sense into his brother and tripped over when his britches slipped down to his ankles," Ivor stated.

George looked at Ivor and burst out laughing.

"This David Jones isn't having much luck, is he!" George said, holding his bruised ribs every time he laughed.

"No, dimwit, it's not all the same man! It's just a popular name around here," Ivor sought to explain, but in so doing only making matters worse.

"These Jones' brothers sound a queer lot!" George gasped, clearly in agony yet unable to stop himself laughing.

"Oh, God, I give up," Ivor said sternly, taking a small cane that was to hand and giving George a few whacks.

After breakfast, George opened his surgery and took delivery of his first patient.

"Right ... um ... Mr Jones, what can I do for you?" George said, beckoning the man into his surgery and gesturing to a chair opposite his desk.

"It's a ewe of mine, Doctor," said Jones, breaking into tears.

"I'm sorry, there appears to have been a bit of a mix-up. I was told you'd a break-up with someone," George said, anxiously thumbing through his paperwork.

"My lovely sheep, Doctor – she's left me!" Jones sobbed. "We first met when she was still a lamb, then again a few years later. I knew then that there was a chemistry between us, and that fate would bring us together. I'll never forget that time our eyes met across that crowded field. That's why I can't believe what she's done to me," Jones said, pausing to wipe the tears from his eyes.

"What has she done?" George asked.

"She's found someone new! A wild-eyed ram," Jones sobbed.

"Well, these things happen and if it wasn't meant to be, it wasn't meant to be," George said. "Perhaps she wanted a family and lambs of her own, maybe a shed in the country. The point is, allow yourself to grieve, but move on. Then if she does come back, it will all be a bonus. No sense in bleating about it," he added.

"Yes, Doctor. I was just wondering if there was something you could give me to help me sleep?" Jones asked, lifting his head and managing a smile.

"Of course," George replied, having already spied a bottle of one of Stumpf's medicines lying in his desk drawer. "Here we are - *Doctor Ronald Stumpf's Patented Universal Panacea - Excellent as a hair restorer, furniture polish, bruise ointment, insect repellent, laxative, purgative, emetic, tooth whitener, enamel cleaner and hair dye. Protects from plague, cholera, anthrax, piles and every other disease or common ailment, including attacks by demons and liberals. Also allows those missing their sheep a good night's sleep*." The last line, of course, was not printed on the bottle, but George had no qualms about telling a little white lie, given that Doctor Stumpf's Universal Panacea would certainly be able to help those missing their loved ones, be they sheep or otherwise.

"I don't know how to thank you, Doctor," Jones said. "And tell Doctor Stumpf my wife says he can come round on Thursday."

"I shall. Does he know why?" George asked.

"Oh yes, it's all in the Bible," Jones explained. "Doctor Stumpf told me that in the Old Testament's Book of Neville, verse two and line twenty it says *And should thy feet be playing-up then thou should let Doctor Stumpf pleasure thy pretty wife whenever he feels a bit randy*. It hasn't stopped my feet playing up but if it's in the scriptures …," Jones said as he stood to leave.

"Ah, I see," said George. "I hope your sheep comes back. Don't forget to invite me to the wedding!" George joked as he watched Jones stand and move to the door.

"Doctor, how's this work then?" Jones asked as he stood at the door.

"Just give the old knob a twist," offered George.

"No Doctor!" Jones said emphatically. "I haven't done that since I was fifteen and started getting hairy palms."

George stood and strode towards the door. He gave the handle a turn, opening the door and letting Jones out.

"Now then, my beauty!" came a loud voice. As the practice door opened and Jones took his leave, a squat man with a mop of greasy hair and cheeks like a bullfrog appeared. Having pushed past the queue and Doctor Mallard, he now strode toward George's surgery door. Ivor did his best to broker an introduction.

"Uh, George, may I introduce you to Mr Eldritch? He supplies many of the better class of Doctors with medicinal materials," Ivor said.

"And bloody good at it as well," boomed Eldritch, laying a hand on George's shoulders and drawing him nearer. "Now come with me," he said, pulling George to the surgery window. "Down there you'll see my brother, behind Mrs Jones and her chickens. You'll notice how handsome he is and what fine legs he has - traits which run in the family! He's what's known as a *Fugger* - he can get you all the latest medical supplies, from dried mummy flesh to petrified frogs. You will notice too that he has a dead body with him. Now dead bodies is dead bodies to most people but to me, they're meat and potatoes. You want some stiffs? I'm your man," Eldritch boasted, then lowered his voice so that the rest of his spiel was inaudible to anyone other than George.

"Well, now that I've introduced you gentlemen to one another, I'll be off," Ivor said timidly, wringing his hands and walking backwards in a half-bowing movement.

"Oh, Mallard, I'm going to be negotiating a little business for a while," said Eldritch. Ivor gave a forced smile that was more pain than pleasure but nodded his agreement.

An hour or so later, Eldritch had concluded his meeting with George and left. George went to his surgery door and spied the waiting room.

"Right then, next please," he said, before sitting at his desk.

"Can I come in then, Doctor?" came a voice from the doorway.

"Of course," said George, looking up to see a pale man making his way to the seat, a mass of bloody blotches under his skin. "Now then, what seems to be the problem, Mr ..."

"Jones. David Jones," said the man. "I just come back from a trip to the Indies, see, and picked up something on board ship," he explained.

George looked at the man and recollected reading something about scurvy. Unfortunately, he'd stopped reading his medical dictionary at *C* but was very good on Alcoholism, Anthrax, Botulism, Burns, the Common Cold, and the Colon. Unfortunately, his diagnosis tended to tail off somewhat once diseases ventured into the *Ds*. Now, what was it that was used to treat the scurvy? George smiled, frowned, looked a little confused and then, enlightened, pointed a few times before checking himself. Finally, he gave a little cough and spoke.

"I think I'd better get a second opinion on this," he said, trying his best to sound as though second opinions were what every Doctor of note was doing this season. George made his way to the door. Striding towards Ivor's room, he listened for voices within and when none came, he opened the door.

"Yes?" said Ivor, quickly turning away from David Jones, the patient with *buckshot in his arse* who now had the pleasure of Ivor gouging out every fragment with his tweezers between puffs on his pipe.

"Oh, nothing. I didn't realise you were busy. I'll go and see Doctor Stumpf," George said, closing the door and making his way to Ronald's room. Again, he paused to listen for voices within and when none came, he entered. Doctor Stumpf quickly fastened his trousers and placed a funnel, length of hose and a bottle of beer in his desk drawer.

"Alcohol never passes my lips," he explained.

"Uh, Doctor Stumpf, I've got a patient - a sailor. I think he might have scurvy. Could you give me a second opinion?" George asked politely.

Ronald, glassy-eyed and grinning, tried to focus.

"George, I've just the thing. I'll be there in a moment," he said, a tone of relish in his voice.

"Thank you," George replied, returning to his surgery.

"Sorry to have kept you," he said to Seaman Jones. No sooner had he spoken, the door of the surgery burst open and in waddled Ronald, cracking a long whip, a look of demonic mania on his orange face.

"Scurvy, eh? I'll give you scurvy! A lick or two of the ship's cat will soon put you right, my boy," he foamed, cracking his whip at both George and Jones as they began yelping and leaping around the room. "Go on, jump!" Ronald shouted, his thrashing becoming ever more frenzied. "I'll soon lash some sense into you! Scurvy? An excuse to laze about drinking rum and fondling other sailors, more like," Ronald added, before moving away from the only door, thus affording George and Jones an exit.

They ran through the waiting room and out of the house. It was only when they were in the street that George sought to compose himself, dusting down his clothes and straightening his neckerchief.

"Right then, Mr Jones, I'm glad we've got a diagnosis," George said, his voice rising in volume as Jones continued his sprint up the street and turning a corner a hundred or so yards away. "Come again soon!"

George turned and took a tentative step back into the house. He had known Ronald to have his *funny ways*, as Ivor had warned him, but he hadn't realised they were quite so pronounced. Imagine being like that! Imagine everyone talking about your odd behaviour! George gave a little shudder and thanked his lucky stars he was so normal.

"Right then, next please," George said, as he walked through the waiting room towards his surgery door. He paused and peered through a small crack where the door had been left slightly ajar. The coast was clear! Ronald, wherever he was, was satisfied now he had thrashed some sense into another work-shy patient.

"You are?" George said, entering the surgery.

"Dai Jones, Doctor," said the man.

"Yes, I rather fancied you might be," George replied. "Now, what seems to be the problem? I'm afraid there have been a few mix-ups today and I don't have your case notes. Doctor Mallard has dealt with quite a few of my patients, as has Doctor Stumpf."

"Well, it's like this, Doctor. I'm broken-hearted, see," Dai Jones began, screwing up his face in misery.

"Go on," George encouraged.

"Well, I think I'm cheating on my wife. What's worse, it's with a male."

George widened his mouth and took an intake of breath.

"Well, if you loved your wife, don't you think you should have been more honest with her?" George asked.

"I would have been, Doctor. I knew it was doomed from the start, but it was love at first sight. It was something about those wild eyes, that dark, firm, fleecy body, that foreign bleat that spoke of far off places ...."

"Sorry, did you say *bleat*?" George interrupted, leaning back in his chair.

"Oh, sorry Doctor, didn't I mention he was a sheep? Yes, Idris has the glossiest coat! He was different from all the other rams I've met. I never thought he'd treat me like this after all I've done for him," Jones mumbled, the memories of stolen moments bringing tears to his eyes. "I'm not a prevert, mind! There was nothing sexy going on. I just found I could talk to him."

"Pervert," George said.

"There's nothing preverted about talking, Doc!" Jones said angrily.

"The word is 'pervert' not 'prevert'," George stammered.

"No! Doctor Stumpf says it's 'prevert' and he knows all the best words."

"Yes, he does. Anyway, back to business! You say Idris left you?" George asked.

"Yes. He said he wanted lambs of his own and ... well, he couldn't ever get that with me, but it didn't bother him when we first met! Now he's run off with some doe-eyed floozy just because she flaunts a well-shaped cloven hoof his way. I always knew he'd leave me one day, but never for a blonde!" Jones sobbed.

"Oh, what a tangled web we weave," George said to himself, thinking how envious Shakespeare would have been if he could have thought of lines like that. If only these sheep had considered the trail of broken hearts they had left in their wake, would they have stopped? Would a sense of shame have called a halt to the pounding of two hearts beating as one?

"Well, you must ask yourself what you got from Idris that you didn't get from your wife," George said sympathetically. "Perhaps if you can put your finger on it, you might be able to make a go of things with her."

"I think that was the problem, Doctor," Jones said.

"What?" George asked, his brow knitting as he wrestled with the point Jones was trying to make.

"My never putting my finger on it," Jones offered.

"Yes, well I'm going to let you have some of this - *Doctor Ronald Stumpf's Patented Universal Panacea - Excellent as a hair restorer, furniture polish, bruise ointment, insect repellent, laxative, purgative, emetic, tooth whitener, enamel cleaner and hair dye. Protects from plague, cholera, anthrax, piles and every other disease or common ailment, including attacks by demons,"* George said, handing Jones a bottle of the same medicine he'd offered the other Jones. "Now you go home and drink some of this," George said, pausing and squinting at the bottle. "Sorry, my mistake! Rub this on the affected areas, and if it's not better in three weeks, perhaps you could make an appointment to see Doctor Stumpf. He's very sympathetic in matters of the heart."

"I still have terrible flatulence, mind. Last time I saw Doctor Stumpf he said my new boots were causing it. I never knew boots could do that but Doctor Stumpf quoted the Book of Colin from the Bible to me as that says 'Should thy suffer from chronic flatulence then thou should give thy new boots to Doctor Stumpf'. That was a couple of years ago and my flatulence is still giving me trouble but it's got to go soon if Doctor Stumpf says it's in the Bible – and he told me that *nobody* reads the Bible more than him."

At last, George had seen his final patient. After the early morning sunshine, there was now a distinct chill in the air and as soon as Jones had left, George moved towards the little coal fire in the back wall of the surgery, throwing a few sticks of wood onto the embers.

As the flames rose, he warmed his hands. Finally, he could relax. Within a minute or so, however, there came a bang at the door and Nurse Conwy entered.

"Hello Nurse Conwy, just uh ... warming my hands," George said nervously, as he rose to his feet and took a few steps backwards.

"Are your hands cold, Doctor? You with such strong Doctor's hands as well! I bet they soon get warm with your bedside manner!" Nurse Conwy said suggestively.

"Uh, no ... not really," George stammered, turning his back on Nurse Conwy and taking a book from a bookcase, a book that he had no intention of reading but which he hoped might give the impression that he was otherwise engaged.

"You could always stick them in my muff," Nurse Conwy offered.

"What! Oh sorry, I thought you meant ... oh, no matter what I thought!" George said, turning quickly to see Nurse Conwy offering a tube of material of the kind ladies of leisure tuck their hands into when the winter chill begins to bite.

"Do you like my muff, George?" Nurse Conwy asked, moving towards George as she spoke. "Slip a few fingers in and feel how warm and soft it is."

"I wanna watch!" Ronald gasped, bursting in and hopping toward them with his britches around his ankles. Both George and Nurse Conwy spun around in surprise, given that neither had known he was within earshot. "Oh, I see, I thought you two were ..." said Ronald, frowning. "I thought I heard someone firing a gun so I sprinted in to see who I could save," he explained, having noticed the small fashion accessory Nurse Conwy was offering George. Without a trace of embarrassment, he bent to pull up his britches before running his hand over a shelf and looked at his fingers, pretending to be looking for dust.

"I've been meaning to have a tidy up," George offered.

"Yes, that was what I came to see you about," Ronald said. "Was there anything else, Nurse Conwy?" he asked, looking in the nurse's direction and arching his eyebrow.

"My hero! You're so brave," Nurse Conwy replied. "I'm going to the market and I wanted to know if anyone wanted anything. I'm after some meat and two veg. Oh, and Doctor Stumpf has just reminded me that I need to get some mushrooms," she added, smiling at Doctor Stumpf and licking her lips before leaving the room.

George gave Ronald an embarrassed look and shrugged his shoulders, feeling self-conscious that Ronald was scrutinising him so intently.

"I've been meaning to ask you, Doctor Stumpf, I've noticed that the old cowshed isn't being used. I also noticed that it has a door straight out onto the street, so I was wondering if I could set up a little laboratory in there to do a few experiments," George inquired.

"Oh yes," Ronald smiled. "Is *that* what they're calling it these days! You must think me and Doctor Mallard to not be men of the world! A little hideaway with a quiet door that goes straight out onto the street, away from the prying eyes of the house? I know your little game!" Ronald said, laughing.

"You do?" George gulped, his eyes bulging.

"Of course. If you're anything like me then you want to entertain ladies down there, don't you?" Ronald said, giving George a playful punch to the chin.

"Oh, you're too smart for me, Doctor Stumpf!" George said smiling, his body slumping as the tension ebbed away. "We're a pair, aren't we Doctor Stumpf!"

"I'm, like, really intelligent," Ronald said. "I'm a very stable genius. You can read all about sex in my book - *The Art of The Feel*. *No one* knows more about sex than me! I do the best sex! As a medical man, I say get in there and get on with it! Don't press *anything* - it's the *Devil's Doorbell*!" he explained.

"Lock up your daughters, eh!" George said, giving Ronald a jovial slap and growling.

"Lock up foreigners!" Ronald replied.

As the two Doctors stood opposite one another, both trying to avoid eye contact and both struggling to find the words to quickly curtail the conversation, a loud rumble of thunder growled, shortly followed by a crackle of lightning and the heavy pitter-pat of rain on the tiles.

"Looks like thunder," Ronald commented making moves towards the door. "I'd better make sure Nurse Conwy has got the washing in."

"Right. Good idea," George enthused as if Ronald's plan of action were somehow exciting.

"Oh! and George," Ronald said, pausing at the door, his hand already on the knob.

"No dancing around on the roof in the nude, eh? We don't want you spoiling our good name and frightening away the patients now, do we?"

"Understood, Doctor Stumpf!" George replied.

"Are you sure?" Ronald laboured, wishing to make his point completely understood.

"No," George replied, a glazed, confused look on his face.

"Look, I don't want you on the roof at all. Not now, not ever," Ronald said.

"Oh right!" George answered, as though the new way of explaining the request had been a revelation. "Sorry, Doctor Stumpf. The wheel's turning but the hamster's dead!"

"Now don't you go trying to change the subject! We were talking about roofs, not hamsters," Ronald said sternly. "Roof, George, no! Understood?"

George raised his hands and gave a thumbs-up. At last, Ronald had made himself understood! Now he could retire for the night, safe in the knowledge that the good name of Mallard, Stumpf and Uppham would remain.

That's a Lovely Looking Leg

Ronald and Ivor gazed out of their old study, through the rain that spattered the leaded window separating them from the outside world, and out onto a lowered section of the roof. Deep rumblings of thunder growled in the distance. Suddenly, a crack of lightning lit up the whole sky for just an instant, capturing the figure of George - naked - as he leapt to and fro on the gleaming wet tiles, his arm stretched high above his head clutching a bolt of metal up to the sky whilst a length of flex trailed across the roof behind him, disappearing from view as it slid off the end of the building.

"Are you sure he's your brother?" Ronald asked.

"Half-brother, please! We have the same father - Sir Richard Uppham - but a different mother. That's why he's thirty years younger than me. If I'd known he was going to be such a ..." Ivor paused and mused carefully before making a choice, "twat, then I wouldn't have agreed to have let him come and practice here."

Suddenly, a second crack of lightning shot across the sky in an eerie blue snap, attacking the end of the rod in the young man's hand with all the ferocity of a snake seizing its prey. Poleaxed, George went rigid and fell from the roof.

There was very little visible reaction to the event from the two Doctors that were watching.

"Are you going to get him?" Ronald asked.

"I suppose I will," said Ivor, running his hands through prematurely white hair. "Little swine," he muttered, as he moved toward the door. Even by dim candlelight he still looked as miserable and unpleasant as he did in broad daylight. As he descended the stairs, the back door burst open and George naked and agitated, jumped in. Static electricity crackled all around him, his hair standing on end.

"Oh, you're alright then?" Ivor asked, not really caring either way.

"Yes, fine," George answered, his teeth chattering so that he was barely comprehensible.

"I still can't believe that you and old Mallard are related," said Ronald, having followed Ivor down the stairs.

"Half-brothers, see!" George said, pointing to a picture on the wall. "Sir Richard Uppham!" he proudly declared. "Our father."

"So, why do you have different surnames if you have the same father?" Ronald asked.

"I can answer that!" Ivor said. "It's the name on the Doctorate I bought from that man in Builth

Wells. Remember? It says my medical Doctorate is in Gastronomy. That's okay, though - if you want your gasterroids looking at. Trust my luck to choose a forger that couldn't spell Gastroenterology!"

"I don't know why you wasted your money," Stumpf said. "Just lie and if anyone asks for proof then move on!"

"You make it sound so easy, Doctor Stumpf!" George gushed, causing Stumpf to shrug his shoulders as though that fact should be a given for he was the chosen one as he could bear the curse of superiority to every other mortal in a way that no one else could, before looking back at the painting on the wall.

"People come up to me all the time and ask me how come I'm so tremendous and I tell them that's it's just the way I am … I'm just very well-endowed," Stumpf explained.

"Anyway, back to the painting. Can't you see the family resemblance?" George said, pulling Doctor Mallard near to him. "Our faces look just like Dick's," George said, pointing at the painting.

"What!" bellowed Ivor. I haven't got a face like a pen … oh, you meant a face like Sir Richard! I thought you meant … well, never mind what I thought," he added, giving a nervous smile. Ronald scowled back, whilst George simply grinned with an expression Ivor hadn't seen since he last took a group of business colleagues on a sightseeing tour around the lunatic asylum. What a day that had been! He hadn't laughed so much since he'd misdiagnosed Iron-Hoof Jones the Blacksmith's plague as hay fever!

"Don't worry Ivor, I won't need to show anyone that painting in the future. I've had a small copy made," George said proudly.

"Have you? Have you?" Ivor answered with savage sarcasm.

"Have you seen it?" George queried.

"Seen what?" Ivor replied, never one to follow the thread of a conversation.

"Have you seen my little Dick Uppham?" George answered.

"What!" Ivor shouted, taking a step back in disgust. "Don't be so foul! Of course, I've never seen your ... oh ... hang on ... yes, of course, you meant the painting. Sorry, I thought you meant ... oh well, no matter what I thought," he added, pretending he'd noticed a particularly interesting mark on the wall and stretching out his hand to smooth it over, thus avoiding eye contact as best he could. Ronald and George looked at one another in bewilderment.

"Anyway, did it work?" said George excitedly.

"Did what work?" Ivor snapped, seeking to overcome his embarrassment by feigning ill-temper.

"Down there," George said, lifting his arm to gesture down the corridor. Unfortunately, his arm had other ideas and flopped towards the floor a few inches up from his wrist, George now finding himself unintentionally pointing at the floor. "Oh, no, not again," he added, fainting into Ivor's outstretched and expectant arms.

When George awoke, he was in bed. Ivor sat pensively in a seat by his side, whilst Ronald stood in the doorway.

"It's a nasty sprain you've got there. Still, at least it's not broken," Ronald said, moving towards the bed and taking hold of George's arm, twisting it into a number of angles, George screaming in agony as various grating and snapping noises came from the arm. "Now tell me, does that hurt?" Ronald asked.

"Honestly?" George asked, trying to smile through the pain. Ronald nodded enthusiastically. "Well, it did smart a bit."

"Then perhaps I ought to do it to your head," Ronald muttered.

"Pardon?" George said.

"Yes, as I thought, it's a nasty sprain."

"Thank God for that," said George. "I thought it might have been broken or something."

"Honestly George! A medical man and you can't even diagnose a sprain! I despair, I really do!" Ivor said, leaning back in his chair and giving a hearty laugh, looking at Ronald in the hope he might join in. Ronald remained stony-faced, however, so Ivor quickly stopped and did his best to show concerned interest. George gave an apologetic smile.

"Sorry, Ivor. I'm just a bit thick sometimes," George admitted, as they were interrupted by a knock at the door.

"*Entrez, mon ami*!" Ivor announced, puffing himself in self-importance as he looked about him for an indication that his French had been impressive. Again, the smile quickly dropped from Ivor's face as he realised no one had paid him any attention. A second knock on the door followed, this time louder.

"Come in!" Ivor said loudly.

"Uh?" the voice from the far side of the heavy door grunted. Ivor stood up and strode purposefully towards it, pausing only to adjust his hair in the small mirror George used for shaving.

"Yes, Nurse Conwy, what is it?" Ivor asked as he pulled the door open, failing to disguise the genuine disappointment he felt when he saw who it was that stood waiting.

"Nothing for you!" she said. "It's for young George. Mr Eldritch is here to see him."

George jumped out of bed, his naked body whirling around the bedroom like a top as he sought some clothes.

"Oh! Doctor George!" said the Nurse, raising her hand to her face in a mock display of shocked virtue, but ensuring she kept her fingers splayed just wide enough to view every inch of the lithe young man in front of her.

"Great!" George enthused, just as the room was darkened by the bulky presence of the visitor. Entering the room loudly, Eldritch knocked George's mirror to the floor and Ivor into the wall, then pointed at George's exposed genitalia and let out a huge laugh that thundered around the small bedroom. All three Doctors strained to follow the direction of Eldritch's outstretched finger, then laughed almost equally as heartily. Only slowly did George realise what the object of their mirth was, his smile turning to a frown.

"I've got some real bargains for you today," said Eldritch, running his fingers-fat-as-sausages through his hair.

"Brilliant!" George shouted, as though all his Christmases had come at once.

Eldritch extended a hand to shake, in a gesture of goodwill. George quickly clasped the hand in his as Eldritch took a jaunty step backwards, leaving George clutching an arm that was severed at the elbow.

"I like to have a laugh," bellowed Eldritch. "As I often say, 'if you can't have a laugh, what can you have?'" he added, looking at Ivor.

"Yes, quite. I was only saying to Ronald this morning. 'Ronald', I said ..."

"Shut up, Mallard. I hate you," shouted Eldritch. Ivor raised both hands and brought his index finger to his pursed lips. If it were silence that was asked for, then it was silence he would get!

"I got a real beauty here!" Eldritch began. "Only planted yesterday and still as stiff as a board. He's a lovely looking fella - nice legs. Then there's old Jumbo Cummings. He stinks a bit - then again, he always did! Dug 'em both up with me own fair hands last night, I did." Eldritch laughed, looking from Mallard to Stumpf. They both laughed when looked at and stopped when the gaze was lost. "I wanted to get old Prong Jones for you, as I thought you'd like something a bit unusual," he added. "Waited bloody years for him, I have, and what does he do? Gets all the way to America and drops dead the first day he's there."

"Lucky swine!" Ivor said. "I wish I could afford to die in America. I can't afford to die down the end of our road."

Ivor's aside was ignored as George and Eldritch began bargaining with one another. Vaguely inquisitive, the naturally gormless expressions of the other two Doctors focussed on Eldritch and the still nude George, as Ivor sidled nonchalantly up to Ronald

"I don't trust that Eldritch. If I didn't know better, I'd swear he's a grave robber," Ivor whispered. Unfortunately for Ivor, his timing could not have been worse as a gap in the conversation between

George and Eldritch allowed the latter to overhear every word.

"What did you say?" Eldritch said, striding towards Ivor, taking a soil-encrusted mattock from beneath his coat as he spoke.

"Ooh, you're in for it now, Ivor!" said George excitedly.

"George! Ronald, say something!" Ivor wailed, beginning to shake.

"Go on, Eldritch. I wouldn't stand for that!" Ronald said, this outburst not being what Ivor had anticipated.

"Oh, I don't intend to. You've done it this time, Mallard. I've always hated you," Eldritch said, taking a swing at Ivor with his mattock, but missing as Ivor ducked.

Ivor jumped onto the bed and dived from there to a corner of the room. Grabbing hold of George's arm, he pulled him close to use as a human shield. The constant to and fro, however, caused George to lose his balance and within a few seconds, he'd fallen face down on the bed, with Ivor on top of him. As they landed, Nurse Conwy returned, only to be greeted by the sight of Ivor on top of his naked brother, both of them sweating, grunting and panting.

"You dirty swine!" she shouted, falling to the floor in a faint. Eldritch grabbed hold of Ivor and, with one flabby left hand, wrenched him free.

"Got you, you little swine! Now, what can I do to a man that casts perspirations on my good name?"

"He could give us a song?" George volunteered.

"George! I'm sure the lovely man can think of something on his own without any help from you," Ivor said.

"No, that's good! I like that. A song is good. Get over there, Mallard," Eldritch barked, pointing to a chair and pushing Ivor toward it. "And if you move, so help me God, I'll take that head off your shoulders, see?" he added, raising his mattock threateningly.

"Uh ... any requests?" asked Ivor nervously, as he sat down.

"Just get on with it!" Ronald interjected.

"Alright! Here goes. Can someone count me in?"

"What a load of rubbish!" George began to chant, Eldritch and Ronald quickly picking up the refrain.

"*I am a little orphan boy, my mother she is dead, My father is a drunkard and won't give me no bread ...*" Ivor began, quickly moving to the end of the sad lament that ended when a chorus of angels came to take the starving child to heaven.

"Hooray, that was brilliant! Give us another, Ivor!" George gushed.

"George, will you shut up! Ronald, can you say something!" Ivor said in desperation.

"Certainly," Ronald replied. "Why don't you sing something we can all join in on? I'm sick of these happy songs. I don't care about starving orphans, I want a sad song about a millionaire losing some of his money."

"Not quite what I had in mind, but thanks for trying," Ivor said sarcastically.

"No! No, that was beautiful! My mother used to sing that to me when I was young," Eldritch said, dabbing his eyes and blowing his nose on the arm of his coat. "Do you know Mallard ... Ivor, in this light you even look a bit like her, save for the moustache, of course."

"I haven't got a moustache," Ivor said, shifting uneasily in his seat.

"Not you, her! I remember it well. My father was so jealous of it. A big black bush of a thing it was. We used to comb food out of it to make soup."

"Uh, I don't want to interrupt anything here, but could I please get up now ... Mr Eldritch ... Sir?" Ivor asked, looking at Eldritch with his large, watery eyes.

"Ah, go on Ivor, give us another first!" George said cajolingly.

"George, will you shut up! Ronald, can't you say something?" By now, Ivor could feel one of his panic attacks coming on, so looked to the elder Doctor for support.

"I could stay here all night," Ronald replied

"Do you know, Doctor, so could I," Eldritch said, looking to the old Quack, his voice tinged with genuine camaraderie.

"Hooray! If only we had some little nibbles or something," George exclaimed, looking around the room as though he were half-expecting to find some.

"Oh good! That's just great then. I'll just sing all night then, shall I?" Ivor said, sinking into his seat.

"I just wish Nurse Conwy were awake to enjoy all the fun," said George as he looked at the unconscious woman lying on the floor. Clearly, the form struck some deep-seated chord inside him, prompting him to rise from his seat and gently tap the woman's face. "No, it's no good, I'll see if I can hear her heart beating," he continued. As George had started his examination while kneeling behind the woman's head, as he leant over to listen for a heartbeat his backside pressed against her face just as she awoke. The unexpected sight at such close range was too much of a shock for her, and she promptly passed out again. "Ah, too bad. Maybe another time," said George, not even aware of the temporary recovery and immediate relapse, as he returned to the edge of the bed.

"Now then," Eldritch continued looking at Ivor coyly. "Mummy sing ickle Eldritch another song ...?"

By the time dawn came the next morning, all four men had fallen asleep. As the sun rose, only Nurse Conwy awoke. Rising to her feet, she gazed around the room.

"Filthy swine," she spat, striding to the door and leaving the room. As she descended the staircase, she paused a moment and flared her nostrils. It only took a moment to recognise the smell of a corpse. As she entered the kitchen, her suspicions were confirmed: two bodies lay on the kitchen table.

Taking a soup ladle down from the wall, she thrust it under the first body's midriff and levered it onto the floor, where it landed with a dull thud. Jumbo Cummins body, however, proved altogether trickier due to its bulk. Eventually, Nurse Conwy despatched him to the floor by lifting one side of the table, so that he rolled, gently at first then gathering momentum like an avalanche of blubber, hitting the floor with less of a thud and more of a splat.

With the table now free of clutter, Nurse Conwy brushed away a few flies then took a lump of meat off a hook above it and dropped it onto the dirty wooden surface, squashing the few flies that remained. Taking a cleaver from a drawer, she wiped the greasy residue from its blade on her dress and proceeded to hack the flesh into lumps.

Noticing that her nails were dirtier than usual, she stopped chopping. With the corner of the cleaver, she scraped the dirt from beneath them, then carried on with her duties. All the exercise, however, caused Nurse Conwy to sweat. Streams began trickling down her face, gathering on the tip of her nose and leaving clean streaks where they had run. As more and more murky beads gathered, they began to drip onto the meat and the table beneath her.

Looking around her for something to jam open the kitchen door, the only things to hand were the bodies. Holding the door open with one hand she manoeuvred one corpse into position with the other, its lifeless head keeping the door ajar.

As the sound of the chopping echoed through the house, three of the four men stirred.

"Now then George, about my bodies ...," Eldritch began.

"I'll take the one with nice legs," George interrupted.

"Tell you what, I'll throw in old Jumbo. How's that? Buy one, get one free!" Eldritch certainly knew how to look after his customers.

Ivor opened one eye, quickly closing it again and pretending to be still asleep. Meanwhile, a sound not unlike tearing sheets erupted from the back of Ronald's britches as he rolled over with a contented look on his face.

Eldritch and George began coughing and spluttering, wiping tears from their eyes as they gasped for breath. Ivor tried his best to control his convulsions, but even after twenty years of flatulent familiarity, he couldn't help but make a series of involuntary retching motions.

"Well George, your bodies are downstairs. That'll be seven guineas for the two," said Eldritch, finally catching his breath.

George moved to his britches and pulled them on, taking a bundle of notes from his pockets.

"Here you are. You're a gentleman and scholar, Eldritch," he said, moving with Eldritch to the door, whereupon Eldritch turned.

"Say goodbye to Ivor for me. Tell him he has the voice of an angel."

"I will, I will. Maybe if you come around later, we'll have another get together."

"I'd like that," Eldritch replied then, once again, pointed at George's groin, laughed at the memory of the night before. George temporarily joined in the fun, then realised what he was laughing at, whereupon the laugh turned to a frown.

As Eldritch's heavy footsteps descending the stairs become less audible, Ivor allowed himself to open both eyes.

"Thank God for that, I thought the fugger would never go!" he growled.

"Ivor!" George shouted in salutation. "You're awake! How's about a little song to start the morni ... " Ivor's foot quickly curtailed the sentence as it connected sharply with George's groin.

"That's for last night as well, you swine!" Ivor said, leaning over George, the latter oblivious to the explanation as he jumped around the room rubbing his genitals.

Around mid-morning, Ronald came into the kitchen with a small pile of dirty underclothes.

"I'm going to boil these," he stated to Nurse Conwy, filling a saucepan with water. "I've had a little accident or two and having scraped off the worst of it, I think a good boil wash should get rid of the rest," he explained.

As Ronald's underwear began to simmer, George, now dressed, came into the room.

"Ah, Nurse Conwy," he said, seeing the nurse busy peeling vegetables "Something smells good," he continued, before taking the ladle and dunking it deep into Ronald's saucepan, then removing it and taking a large gulp. "Mmm, soup," he said. "Unusual flavour though - very gamey."

Later that day, Ivor paid a visit to George's cowshed-cum-laboratory where the two bodies now lay motionless on planks of wood that, in turn, rested on milk churns, thus bringing the bodies to waist height. All the while, pigs, chickens and sheep wandered back and forth.

"Christ, George, it stinks in here! Why don't you get rid of the pig for a start?" Ivor gasped, burying his face in his arm.

"Get rid of him! I've only just brought him in here! You should have smelt it before!" George said, hardly taking his eyes from his work.

"I've been meaning to ask you, George, why do you run around the roof in the nude every time we have a thunderstorm?" Ivor asked, taking a large draw on his old clay pipe, lit in the hope of masking the odious smell.

"It's the Enlightenment, Ivor. Things are changing. Galvani and electricity and all that. I'm trying to capture power from a bolt of lightning," George answered, removing his hands from the open stomach of a cadaver and wiping them on his coat.

"One question, George - why?" Ivor asked, distinctly unimpressed by George's reason.

"It's a new age, Ivor. A new era. An era of optimism. Electricity can do anything!" George enthused, just as the surgery dog, Himbry – no one knew from where the name had come - leapt alongside the open body and dipped his head into the hole, drawing forth a considerable length of intestine and making a bolt for the door with it.

"Hey, come back! I wanted that, you little swine!" George shouted, setting off in hot pursuit. It was, however, too late as the dog was gone in a black and-white-mongrel-type flash, along with the insides of the corpse.

"Sorry about that, Ivor," George said, returning empty-handed. "Oh yes, as I was saying, electricity will be the power of the future," George continued, returning to the body to see exactly what the dog had pilfered.

"Oh really! Such as?" Ivor had suspected his brother of being stupid, but then he couldn't be that stupid, could he?

"Oh, I don't know," George answered, struggling to think of an example now he had been put on the spot. "Power a lamp so that a house might be as bright by night as it is by day. Start a heart beating again." George felt sure that would convince his older brother.

"George, George, George, George, George, you poor misguided fool! You really talk some complete balls at times. I mean, what next? Listen to Doctor Stumpf when he says that we should all go with gut instinct rather than science. You'll be telling me that ....." Ivor paused and drew the pipe away from his mouth to think of an example. "Yes, you'll be telling me next that tobacco is bad for children," he added, laughing.

"Really, Ivor! That would be stupid. Everyone knows tobacco is good for you! That's the trouble with you - you always have to exaggerate things fifty million times. I'm telling you, electricity will be the power of the future."

"Look, we all know windmills give you cancer - we don't need science to prove it! Just go with your gut instinct, like Doctor Stumpf," Ivor added. Suddenly, a sight from the window distracted him. "Look, there's Mrs Jones! Mrs Jones!" Ivor shouted, leaning from the window and waving. "Do you know, every time I see that woman she has a cock in her hand!" he said, taking a step back into the room

"What!" George said excitedly, rushing to the window. "Oh, a chicken! I thought you meant ... oh, never mind what I thought," he added, unable to conceal his disappointment.

Suddenly, there was a knock at the door.

"Who's that? You expecting someone?" asked Ivor nervously.

"It's for you!" George replied, lifting the arm of one of the bodies and waving it in Ivor's direction.

"Will you stop messing about? It could be Ronald back from Cardiff with those tapered leeches I ordered," Ivor answered, moving to the window and trying to peer out without being seen.

"Tapered?" George asked.

"Yes, it makes them easier to insert," Ivor answered from the corner of his mouth.

George nodded as though he understood then abruptly stopped, his face registering alarm as the implication of what his brother had said dawned on him.

"It's that fugging madman Eldritch," Ivor said.

"Eldritch?" George looked confused and began rolling his eyes and biting his lip.

"Yes, George, Mr Eldritch," said Ivor, recognising the look on George's face as one of blind ignorance.

"Now I know this. Oh, don't tell me. It's coming. It's coming." There followed a long pause during which George screwed up his eyes and shook his head from side to side, as though he were telling some unseen friend *no*. "No, Ivor, I give up. You're going to have to tell me."

"Eldritch! The man who gave you the stiffs last night!" Ivor said in desperation. George let out a shocked gasp and took a step backwards.

"Don't be so disgusting! No man has ever given me the stiffs! I certainly wasn't with any rough trade last night. Last night I listened to you singing." Suddenly, a look of illumination spread across his face, as though somebody had blown away the clouds inside his head, allowing the sun to shine through. "Oh, *that* Eldritch! Cuh, sometimes I'm so stupid I think I must be the stupidest man in um ... uh ... um ..."

"Wales?" Ivor offered.

"That's it! Wales. I'm useless with those long names," George confessed. A second, fiercer, bang echoed through the little room.

"That's it, I'm off. He's all yours," Ivor said, running for the door that led back to the house. George moved to the door Eldritch was loudly banging and swung it wide open on its rusting strap hinges. No sooner had he done so than Eldritch strode in, replete with corpse.

"I've another beauty for you here," Eldritch gasped, unloading the body next to the two he'd brought the night before. "Lovely legs," he continued, rolling down the corpse's stockings. "Go on, have a feel. Lovely they are and still warm, too."

George meanwhile, having moved around the corpse, had stopped at the man's face. Crouching down, he frowned as though lost in thought.

"I don't wish to be too picky, Eldritch, but this man is breathing," George said awkwardly, fearing Eldritch's reaction.

"Trick of the light. He's dead alright."

"I could have sworn I saw him breathing."

"Well, you're the Doctor. Check him over - if you don't believe me, that is."

George hated confrontations and now embarrassed that he had doubted the word of his fugging friend, he took a deep intake of breath.

"No, that won't be necessary. If you say he's dead then I'm sure he is."

"Tell you what," Eldritch said. "If it will make you feel any better, give me five minutes alone with him and I'll make sure he's dead."

For a moment, George was taken in by the tone of Eldritch's persuasive argument and even considered thanking him for his kind offer.

"No, Eldritch, you can't kill him. Besides ..." George took another look at the man's face. "Eldritch, isn't this your brother? I'm sure he's that fugger I saw from the window."

There followed a long pause in which Eldritch looked awkward. He rubbed his fat belly then placed an index finger on the table, casually twisting it from side to side as he cast his eyes to the ground.

"Could be," he admitted. Feeling braver now that the admission was out, he added "Oh, so what if he is! He *is* dead, I promise you!"

George was now beginning to waver. He had another look at the corpse's face and placed his head against its chest.

"I promise you, fit as a fiddle he was. Just this morning he came home for a bite to eat and keeled over. No use being sentimental, I thought, not when there's rent to be paid. Besides, legs like this can fetch a good price."

"I think I'd better let my colleagues have a look if you don't mind," George said, moving to the door and calling to his fellow practitioners. Soon, Ivor came into the room, closely followed by Ronald, who had by now returned with the leeches.

"I'm having a little difficulty diagnosing death. What do you two think?" George asked.

Ivor sank his hands deep into his britches pockets and nudged Ronald, nodding at George as he did so, his wry smile seeming to say *can you believe this?* Ronald's stony grimace remained impassive. Ivor immediately lost his smile and feigned a serious and concerned look as a result.

"Oh yes. Clearly dead," Ronald said, whilst still a considerable distance from the body.

"He is, Doctor - drank himself to death," Eldritch offered, as Ronald moved towards the corpse.

58

"Oh yes, dead alright. Look, he's stiff as a ... board." Ronald lifted the body's arm, only for it to limply flop from his grasp.

"It's like this, Doctor. He died in a fire, see. Flames must have kept him warm, that's why he's not as stiff as he should be," Eldritch suggested, looking at Ivor, who nodded in agreement.

Suddenly, the corpse let out a loud snore. All three Doctors turned to face Eldritch.

"The death rattle!" Eldritch stuttered.

"Ah, yes. That explains it. Although ..." Ronald moved forward to open the corpse's eye. "Ah, damn you! Damn your eyes! Cursed! Cursed I am! It's the evil eye! The evil eye!" he screamed, as he ran from the room.

"Well, I'm glad we cleared that little problem up. If you need any more professional advice, George, please let either myself or Doctor Stumpf know," Ivor said, just as a pig in the corner of the room grunted loudly, drowning out the last of his words. Ivor turned tail and with all the professional air he could muster, strode towards the door left ajar by Ronald's hasty departure. However, the dignity of his departure was punctured by his treading in a little deposit left by the aforementioned pig and skidding through the open doorway, colliding into the wall opposite and disappearing from view.

Later that night George was hard at work and all alone in the cowshed. He had persuaded his brother to bandage up his arm and, loaded on laudanum, he whirled feverishly around the glut of bodies about him. Exposing the leg of the latest arrival, he took a step back in mute admiration. "What a work of art," he mused. With a slow method, he moved to the corner of the room to fetch his sharpest saw. He bent the blade as though he were flexing a rapier. The blade sprang from his grasp and knocked him in the face.

"I promise you, this is going to hurt you a lot more than it hurts me," George said to the corpse, wiping the blood from his nose. In the dim light, he dug his fingers into the flesh to find the exact centre of the knee and began to saw, slowly at first, then faster as the blade sank deeper and deeper into the soft tissue.

"Oh, God, my bloody leg!" came a voice from under the blanket George had used to cover the corpse.

"Who said that?" George stammered, his eyes rolling cautiously around the room. He'd read his Vathek and his Castle of Otranto and now he half expected a ghostly hand to appear suspended in the gloomy room, or some dreadful spectre to come from hell to punish him for his diabolism. There was no reply to his question, so nervously he began sawing again.

"Oh, God, that smarts," came the voice, just as George cut through the last of the leg and brought it away. Suddenly, the body beneath the sheet sat bolt upright.

"Argh!" shrieked George, dropping the leg and fleeing to the warm refuge of the house.

"Argh! Oh, God! I swear I'll never touch another drop. My head feels like death. What the fu ...?" As might have been expected, Eldritch Junior quickly realised he was minus a leg, despite the copious amounts of gin with which Eldritch senior had plied him. Sliding from the table, he hopped to the door and away into the night.

Meanwhile, the leg had not gone unnoticed. Himbry, the surgery's mongrel-cum-intestine thief, casually strolled up to it. Now, this was a new treat! Smelling the foot, he closed his eyes in ecstasy and began to lick between the sweaty toes.

"Quick, Ivor. You're not going to believe it. I've perfected the art of resurrection! I, George Uppham, have found a way to re-animate the dead!" George shouted defiantly as he burst into the surgery's living quarters, as though he had fought and won the age-old battle of life and death.

Ivor lifted himself from his comfy chair and put his hot buttered crumpets next to his tea on the tray beside him.

"George, please calm yourself. Now, what was that you said? You've found a way of re-animating the dead?" he said, pausing only to smirk. "So, you, George Uppham, have found the Philosopher's Stone - the key to immortal life?" he asked, sinking his hands into his pockets and looking at Ronald, nodding towards George as he spoke. Ronald remained stony-faced; Ivor, too, quickly losing his smile and drawing his hands from his pockets. "George, I want you to answer me truthfully - have you been drinking Doctor Stumpf's liniment rub?"

"Not this time, Ivor ... cuh! Not after last time," George smiled, rolling his eyes to the back of his skull at the memory.

"I have, and the leeches," belched Ronald, lying prone on the sofa.

"What! You've been eating the leeches?" Ivor was almost speechless at the confession, looking at George to confirm the astonishment was not misplaced.

"Anyway, Ivor ..."

"Yes, sorry George, you were saying. Oh yes, might one ask how this miracle was achieved?"

"Witchcraft. Devil's work. He'll burn for it! Look for the witch's mark - give him a good pricking," Ronald mumbled, the rest of his sentence becoming incoherent as he passed out.

"A 'pricking'?" queried George.

"It's not what you think, as I used to think the same! It's what they used to do to find a witch. Prick them until they found a spot insensitive to pain. That's where the Devil was thought to have made his mark on them," Ivor explained.

"I knew all that. What did you think I thought?" asked George.

"Um ... oh look, it doesn't matter," Ivor replied, feeling his cheeks burning where he'd stood with his back too close to the fire.

"Yes, I cut off that man's leg and he came back to life just as I'd finished," George enthused.

"Oh, that's just marvellous! George, you've resurrected a corpse! Don't you think he's going to be seriously pissed off when he realises that he's one leg short of a pair? Were you hoping he wasn't going to notice? Think of the problems he's going to have!"

George looked perplexed, his face running the gamut of emotions from A to B as he wrestled with the problem.

"It's not all bad," George finally acknowledged.

"Not all bad! I don't believe this. George, how bad do you want it to be? We've got a resurrected corpse hopping around on one bloody leg! How bad can it get?" Ivor allowed himself to slump into his chair and buried his face in his hands.

"It could be worse!" George stammered, desperate to win Ivor's enthusiasm.

"How?" Ivor leaned back in his seat and folded his arms in superior resignation. "Give me one positive aspect."

George paused, making three false starts at an answer, pointing with his finger each time an answer seemed about to arise, before checking himself.

"He'll save a fortune at the cobblers," was the best he could finally manage.

"Yes, yes he would," said Ivor reflectively. "I'd not thought of that. Yes, he would save a bit of money there."

"Mind you ..." interrupted George.

"What?" asked Ivor gravely.

"My money wouldn't be on him in an arse-kicking contest."

"George," said Ivor. "Just show me the leg."

Back in the cowshed, George and Ivor moved with trepidation across the straw-strewn floor.

"Watch out for the cowpats," George advised, as Ivor slid silently to the floor after treading in a particularly large one. Turning, and expecting to see his brother close behind him, George took a large gulp. The corpse had already taken Ivor and now it would be after him! Oh, God, he was sorry! Then cold clammy hands began wrapping themselves around his ankle.

"Argh!" he screamed.

"Argh!" screamed Ivor.

"Oh, God, it's you, Ivor! You frightened the life out of me. I thought it was ... him," George said, looking around the room. "Why are you lying on the floor? I wouldn't lie down there. Not with all those turds about."

"George! I wasn't lying. I slipped over. Now can we please take a look at this leg."

"Here it is," said George, stopping to pick up the leg. "Oh, no! The dog has only gone and had the toes. I knew I shouldn't have left it on the floor," he added, handing the leg to his brother.

"Still, no matter," said Ivor, taking it into the light. "That's a lovely looking leg, I'll say that much. George, do you know what this means? It means we can bring back anyone we want just by cutting off their leg!" Already Ivor could feel his wallet bulging with the cash such a scheme could extort from the rich and famous.

"But you said ..." George began, confused by his brother's about-turn.

"George! Never mind what I said. I've changed my mind."

Like an explosion, a clap of thunder preceded the heavy patter of rain on the slate above their heads.

"Sorry Ivor," said George smiling. "I've got to ... take a pee. Ivor watched suspiciously as George skipped out of the room. Lost in fantasies of wealth, Ivor followed him, unaware that he was still clutching the leg.

George leapt around the roof in the heavy rain and crashing thunder. Nonchalantly, Ivor watched from the study window, lost in a greedy reverie. Without thinking, he scratched the back of his head with the remnants of the leg. Then, as one might take a pen, he began to tap his chin with the foot, pondering what his first acquisitions would be if he were rich. Almost before he knew it, he'd begun chewing and sucking on the foot. The taste suddenly set off some deep-seated alarm bells in his head and his conscious mind sprang to the fore.

"Oh, God!" he cried in disgust, taking a step backwards and pulling the leg far away from his face as he tried to spit out the taste. As it slowly faded, Ivor brought the leg slowly back up to his face. Had it really been as vile as he'd imagined? Flaring his nostrils, he took a little sniff - nothing. Bringing the foot a little nearer, he flared his nostrils again and took a deep snort. Vile wasn't the word! The terrible smell of strong cheese on a hot summer's day didn't so much waft up his nasal passages as take them in a strong grip and throttle them. Ivor retched as he looked through the window, just in time to see his brother plummet from the edge of the roof and disappear into the darkness.

"Twat!" he shouted, tossing the leg to one side and drawing on his coat to mount the rescue bid that had become the expected climax to every stormy night.

Ivor carried the dazed body of his brother to his room and placed him on the bed, before retiring for the night.

When Ivor awoke next morning, the house was curiously silent. He quickly dressed and made his way to George's room, where the door was open. Inside, Nurse Conwy stood to one side whilst Ronald sat in a chair conducting a diagnosis

"Well, Doctor?" Ivor asked.

"Dead of course. I knew it! It'll soon be us, you know. It was the forces of darkness and the evil eye. Look, he's even got three nipples," Ronald said pulling back the sheets to expose a dry, flattened, piece of indiscernible food clinging to George's chest.

"What do we do then, Doctor? We don't want him smelling up the house," asked Nurse Conwy, wringing her hands. "At least, not any more than when he was alive."

Ivor looked at George in the bed, and in particular at his brother's chest as it steadily rose and fell as he breathed in and out.

"Are you sure he's dead, Ronald? It looks like he's breathing to me," Ivor said, taking a step backwards as he spoke, pre-empting Ronald's hostile reply.

"Of course he's dead! The little swine's as dead as a doornail," Ronald shouted, standing up and throwing his medical tools to the floor in a rage. "The movement you see is the humours. That'll be his phlegm."

"Phlegm? It looks like he's got a lot in there, what with his whole chest moving up and down," Nurse Conwy said.

"It's the phlegm! If I say it's the phlegm, it's the phlegm! *Nobody* knows more about phlegm than me!" Ronald shouted, stamping his foot and waving his arms, as though he were a mad Roman orator.

"Well, if it's all the same to you, Doctor, I'll just stand a bit away from him then. There must be a gallon of the stuff in there and I'm not catching it should the little swine sneeze," Nurse Conwy said, taking a few tentative steps backwards.

"What do we do now then, Ronald?" Ivor asked.

"Uh?" Ronald grunted as he turned to face Ivor.

"Well, as I see it, we have three options - we can bury him, sell him to Eldritch, or cut off his leg and bring him back from the dead," Ivor posited.

"What!" shouted Ronald.

"Bury him then?" Ivor asked, taking a second step backwards and giving a supplicating smile.

"No, sell him to Eldritch of course!" Ronald answered, barging past Ivor, evidently in pursuit of the filthy lucre that could be obtained from a fresh young corpse.

Within a few minutes, Ronald returned with Eldritch who, to everyone's astonishment, was openly weeping.

"Oh, God, no! I don't think I can go on," Eldritch began, then broke into violent sobs, throwing himself to the side of the bed and taking George in his arms.

"I must say, Eldritch, I'm touched. Here we all were thinking you nothing more than a fat, money-grabbing git willing to sell his own brother - who *did* sell his own brother, come to think of it - when all along you really do have a soft spot in that heart of stone of yours," Ivor said, dabbing a tear from his eye. "There, there, Mummy make it better," he continued, patting Eldritch's huge back as it went into paroxysms of uncontrollable grief. Eldritch temporarily stopped crying and looked up, his puffy eyes a bloodshot red.

"Do I balls! He was my best customer! I don't know what I'm going to do without his cash," Eldritch answered, turning back to George and violently shaking him. "Wake up! Wake up, you swine! You still owe me some money for that liver I sold you. Who's going to keep me in gin and filthy woodcuts now?"

"So, Eldritch, will you give us cash for the stiff?" Ronald interjected.

"What! Doctor Stumpf, please! My brother's lying dead and all you can think about is sex ... oh sorry, I thought you meant ... oh well, it doesn't matter what I thought," Ivor said, burying his red face in the arm of his coat and pretending to cry, only stopping when he thought the moment had passed and nobody was looking at him.

"Uh?" Eldritch said, standing up and doing some calculations in his head as he pondered Ronald's request.

"I guessed the thought of some easy money might change things Eldritch, you disgust me!" Ivor said with contempt.

"Two pounds and six shillings," Eldritch answered, ignoring Ivor's insults.

"Two pounds and six shillings!" Ivor shouted enthusiastically. "Fantastic!" He linked arms with Ronald and danced around the room.

"Right then, I'll just have him away. Luckily, I've brought my bag with me," Eldritch said, pulling a rough hessian sack from some deep pocket and unfurling it on the bed. With little ceremony, he scooped up his former customer and dropped him into the bag. "My, he is a big one," he added, realising George's feet protruded from the open end.

Quickly, Eldritch hoisted the sack over his shoulder and, after counting out some notes and coins, strode into the street with the bag in full view.

"Morning, Bill. What's in the sack?" asked a local, as Eldritch walked confidently down the cobbled street.

"Sack? What sack?" Eldritch asked, looking around as though he were expecting to see one on the floor or being carried by someone else.

The man took a step closer and tugged at Eldritch's sack, then took hold of the hessian bag and gave that a tug as well. The bag let out a low groan and began to move.

"Oh, *that* sack! It's a … um … a Mexican.".

"A what! I've never been to Mexican and if what Doctor Stumpf says is true I never will!" said the old man, beating the sack with his walking stick until he was breathless. "Thank you, Bill", he continued. "Doctor Stumpf was right! That really has made me feel so much better about myself."

"My pleasure," said Eldritch.

"By the way, Bill, where is Mexican?"

"Um … near Aberystwyth."

"Well, I certainly I won't be going there, then!" said the local, as he sauntered off with a spring in his step.

As Eldritch reached some woodland, the sack let out a second protracted groan. Eldritch looked around, unnerved and confused as to where the noise was coming from. Suddenly, the sack moved and, tearing a hole in the fabric, George pushed his head through the narrow slit.

"Hello, Eldritch!" he said, in his usual cheery manner.

Shaken, Eldritch dropped the sack and took a few steps backwards. George quickly freed himself from the bag and stood up, offering an outstretched hand to the quaking graverobber. Terrified, Eldritch clutched at his chest, went a curious colour and collapsed.

George rushed to Eldritch. After rolling the blubbery mass over, he looked furtively around then rolled Eldritch into the bag. Failing to lift the enormous weight, he began dragging the sack of limp flesh home.

Back at the house Ronald and Ivor relaxed in their living room, Ronald soundly asleep and snoring loudly whilst Ivor simply reminisced.

"You know, I'll miss young George," he said, looking at Ronald who, as if on cue, let out an enormous window-rattling snore. "Nice to know it's resting so heavily on your heart! You know, I should have cut off his leg when I had the chance. He'd be here now if I had. Then I'd have had someone to talk to! Still, if he were here, I wouldn't have you, would I, my beauties!" he added, looking to his side and patting a dozen bottles of whiskey.

Interrupting the tranquil scene came a tap at the window.

"Who ... who's there?" Call it guilt or remorse, but Ivor sensed his brother would come back to haunt him.

"Ivor, it's me - George," George said, pressing his face against the glass.

Ivor looked towards the ceiling, expecting to see some spirit hovering around the room.

"George? George, is it really you? Oh, George, I'm sorry I didn't cut off your leg when I had the chance. It was Ronald! Ronald made me do it. He said to sell you. Oh, George, please forgive me! If you want to haunt anyone, haunt him," he cried pointing at Ronald asleep on the sofa.

"Eh? I can't hear you," answered George, pressing his ear to the glass.

"I said ... oh look, it doesn't matter. Oh, George, what can I do for you so that your unquiet spirit might find some peace in its lonely wanderings?"

"You can let me in. I have a heavy weight on my shoulders."

"Alas, as you did in life, you poor, poor child," Ivor sobbed.

"You've got to let me in. I've nowhere else to go!"

"Oh, George, don't say such things! Can you find no peace anywhere? I know you were never a saint, but I didn't think they'd deny you entry to everlasting glory! Still, at least it's not ... down there," Ivor said, lowering his eyes to the floor then screwing them tightly shut and clasping his hands together as if in prayer.

"Look, can you just open the door?" By now, George was beginning to lose his patience.

"Oh, God, I'm sorry, I'm so sorry. Ronald, wake up," Ivor wailed, running over to the prone form and shaking him. "Wake up, you lazy twat!" Ivor took a step backwards and stumbled on an empty jar. Picking it up, he squinted as he read the label: Liniment Rub.

"You ..." Ivor clutched hold of Ronald's neckerchief, raising a fist in front of his face as if to punch him. "You haven't been boofing this, have you?" Suddenly, there was a shattering of glass and George entered, complete with sack, scraping to a slow stop as George released his grip on his weighty burden with a relieved sigh.

"Hello Ivor!" he said, enforcing the greeting with a cheery wave.

"Argh!" Ivor screamed, diving for safety behind the sofa. As the noise rang out, the sack let out a mighty groan and Eldritch sat bolt upright.

"Argh!" George screamed, joining Ivor behind the sofa.

"Right, you shower of swine," Eldritch shouted, as the two Doctors looked up to see his corpulent form standing over them. "Now, where's my mattock? I can feel a little sing-song coming on!"

Ahoy There, Maties!

By the time morning came, Eldritch had both George and Ivor harmonising and even singing counterpoint with one another but having become bored he'd fallen asleep.

"Here's our chance, Ivor," said George.

"Chance to do what?"

"Knock him on the head," George suggested, lowering his voice.

"Oh great! Good one, George! What do you propose we do then? We knock him on the head and then we either have a blubbery corpse to dispose of - with no buyers! - or a very irate madman with a lump on his head," Ivor said, raising his eyes to the ceiling in disgust. "No, we need to think this thing through."

"Throw him in the river?" George said excitedly, as though the perfect plan had just come into his head.

"George, just when I think you can't get any more stupid, you go and say something like that! That's brilliant!" Ivor said.

"So, will you knock him on the head, or shall I?" George queried.

"You can. I'll just stay over here and make sure nothing goes wrong," Ivor said, taking a few steps backwards.

"Right then. Wish me luck, I'm going in," George said, standing behind the sleeping Eldritch and lifting his arm high above his head. As he did so, Ivor winced and looked away. For a while, there was silence. Ivor opened his eyes, leaping backwards at the sight of George's face just a few inches away from him.

"What is it?" Ivor said, holding his chest in fright.

"I haven't got anything to hit him with," George replied, a sheepish smile spreading across his face.

"Oh look, this is ridiculous," Ivor said, pushing George out of the way. "If you want anyone killed, you've got to do it yourself," he moaned, moving behind Eldritch, taking a full bottle of whiskey from his cache as he went.

"Right, you stand there," Ivor said, pointing to an area a few feet in front of the sleeping man. "Now, when I hit him, you make sure nothing goes wrong. If he's not out cold with the first blow, we're in big trouble," Ivor said.

"Right you are," George said, bracing himself.

Ivor raised the bottle high above his head and, closing his eyes, brought it down with all the force he could muster on the top of Eldritch's head. Immediately, the sleeping man awoke and leapt from the chair.

"Quick, get him," Ivor shouted, taking a few steps backwards.

"Die, you swine!" George rasped, jumping at Eldritch and wrapping his hands around the fat throat of the dazed fugger.

"Go on, George, you've got him on the ropes! He's weakening," Ivor encouraged, as Eldritch staggered around the room with George clinging to his throat like an ineffectual scarf.

"The bottle! Use the bloody bottle!" George shouted. Ivor didn't need telling twice and tossed the bottle at George who, otherwise engaged, was in no position to catch it.

"Well, you might have made some effort to catch it!" Ivor remonstrated.

"Just kill the bugger!" George shouted, even more fearful now he realised that Eldritch had begun to notice what was going on and was now directing his attention at George.

Ivor grabbed a second bottle from his hoard and took a step forward, striking out with eyes closed. The resounding thump told him that this time he had been successful.

"That was a close one!" George said when the heaving mass of flesh lay between the two of them.

"George, *Die, you swine*? *Kill the bugger*? I must confess, such sentiments stand in stark contradiction to your status as a medical man," Ivor remarked.

"It's like this, Ivor," George said, wiping the sweat from his brow. "If a Doctor's mandate is to prolong life and ease suffering, I've just done both. The fact that the suffering we've eased and the life we've prolonged are ours and not the patient's is but a minor technicality," George observed.

"Very good, George! And that's our defence, is it?" Ivor said, folding his arms haughtily.

"That's your defence. You killed him!" George answered, collapsing in a chair.

"You conniving swine!" Ivor shouted, taking a step towards George and angrily pointing at him.

"Hang on! You forget the second part of our fiendishly clever plan. We're going to throw him in the river, remember?"

"Brilliant!" Ivor said, clapping his hands together and smiling.

"What's going on?" Ronald said, awaking and shaking his head as he sought solace from his hangover.

"It's Eldritch. He's dead and ... uh ... you killed him!" Ivor said. "Isn't that right, George?"

"I killed him? God, I really must stop boofing!" Ronald said, running his hands through his hairpiece.

"Yes, Ivor and I tried to stop you but you had bloodlust in your eyes," George said, warming to Ivor's story.

"I can't remember a thing! I remember hearing these two awful voices singing, but nothing else. Are you sure I killed him? I might have done. I never liked him. He was the first person to ever throw a leg at me," Ronald said.

"Well, there you are then! I knew there must have been a motive. A reasonable man like you doesn't go around killing just anyone," Ivor said, nodding at George to back up the story.

"Ivor and I thought it would be a good idea if you threw him in the river," George added.

"Yes, thank you, George. But of course, we didn't know he'd been killed, did we, as we've only just come into the room, remember?" Ivor hissed through gritted teeth.

"Oh, yes ... we knew nothing about it and weren't even here ... at all. In fact, we were out and the first we knew about it was when ..."

"Yes, thank you Doctor Uppham. I'm sure Doctor Stumpf doesn't want all the details, given he's still coming to terms with the terrible knowledge that he's a murderer," Ivor said, kicking George on the ankle.

"Oh, that doesn't worry me. I just sell them to Mrs Jones at the butcher's to make sausages. Trouble is, she only likes lean meat and there's too much fat on him ..." Stumpf began before Ivor interrupted.

"Mrs Jones at the butchers? Mrs Jones as in *the* Mrs Jones from Jones Street?" he asked, the colour draining from his face.

"Yes, that's the one. Do you know her?" Stumpf asked.

"Not as a patient, but I buy my sausages from her!" Ivor said, slumping into a chair. George laughed, pointed at Ivor and made a few retching motions.

"I don't know what you're laughing at, halfwit, you don't think I buy your sausages from a different butcher's do you?" Ivor remarked.

"Oh, no!" George wailed, his laughter stopping in an instant.

"Ronald, please tell me you only sell the attractive bodies to Mrs Jones. I hope that old choleric who pegged out last week didn't go," Ivor pleaded. Ronald shrugged his shoulders and closed his eyes.

"Now if it had been that young Miss Jones who stiffed when I was last here," George said, closing his eyes and smacking his lips, whilst rubbing his belly.

"I need two scoops of ice cream while I think this through," Ronald said, racing from the room.

"Give me a hand to get fatty to the river then," said Ivor, leaving the room for a few moments before returning with half a roll of sacking and a small trolley that had accidentally been left behind when they had once had a piano delivered.

The journey to the river was uneventful, but after heaving the bulk from the bridge, the two Doctors watched in dismay as instead of sinking, the body floated down the river like a dry log.

"Of course! All that fat doesn't sink, does it?" George said, slapping his forehead with the palm of his hand.

"Excuse me?" came a voice behind the duo.

"It wasn't me! He made me do it!" George gabbled, pointing at Ivor.

"I do beg your pardon but you seem to have misunderstood me. My name is Lindsey Grayson. I'm a special friend of Ronald Strumpfhosen's," said the man, dabbing his lips with a handkerchief.

"Strumpfhosen? I don't think I know him. We're Doctor Stumpf's partners, Ivor said.

"Both of you! How positively Romanesque!" Lindsey exclaimed, his lips pursing and eyes widening.

"Ronald's a one, isn't he? His mind's never off the job! He's always ready to get down to a bit of business," George gushed.

"He certainly has some special qualities," Lindsey replied, his eyes twinkling.

"We're going back to the house now so you might as well come with us," George said.

"Are you sure? I don't want to tread on anyone's toes. Jealousy is such a beastly thing, don't you think? One can hardly think of it without having to have a lie down."

"Yes, we're all a bit like that, aren't we, Ivor? If it wasn't for the patients, I think the three of us would stay in bed all day!" George laughed.

"I can see I'm going to enjoy it here," Lindsey said, drawing his fingers slowly up and down his thick ebony cane.

Back at the house, there was no sign of Ronald.

"I'll go and see if I can rouse Ronald for you," George said, mounting the stairs and making his way to Ronald's surgery. The door was slightly ajar, so George pushed it a little and entered.

"Doctor Stumpf, there's a visitor for you."

"A visitor? I'm not expecting anyone," Ronald said, frowning and trying to swallow his ice cream. "Did you get a name?"

"Lindsey Grayson," George offered.

"Doesn't ring any bells" Ronald scowled. "Is he a salesman or something?"

"At first I thought he was just a friend of yours, but I think he might be a salesman."

"Why, what is he selling?" Ronald queried.

"Toilets, I think. On the walk back to the house he mentioned to Ivor and me that he was a toilet trader," George answered.

Ronald, his mouth full of ice cream, sprayed a plume of it into the air on hearing George's words.

"Yes, I think you must have gone to an exhibition or something, as he said he met you and Father Catamite at the same time. To tell you the truth," George continued, "I don't blame Father Catamite for looking for a nice toilet - the number of times I've seen him in and out of that toilet in the town, I swear he must have the weakest bladder in Wales! Strange how he's never come to us to get some treatment for it," he pondered aloud.

"Alright, thank you, George, that will be all. If you could show my friend Lindsey up," Ronald said.

"Of course," George replied, leaving Ronald and returning to the reception room where Ivor had left Lindsey.

"I see you enjoy the finer things in life," Lindsey remarked upon George's return.

"Eh?" George replied.

"The painting, my pale Narcissus, the painting!" Lindsey said, gesturing to a canvas on the wall.

"Oh yes. There's nothing I like better than getting down to business with a few oils," George replied.

"Me too! A beautiful painting in the classical style transports me to far-off places and far-off times where a spiritual union was not a sin. Nothing gives me greater pleasure than the sight of a marble-skinned youth resting his weary head against a Doric column or two, what do you say?"

"Yes. Have you seen our books?" George replied, a little confused.

"Oh, I have, I have! Just before you returned, I had William Beckford in my hand but he became rather moist so I had to put him down," Lindsey said.

"Right. Anyway, I've spoken with Doctor Stumpf and he'd like to see you. I think he might be able to put some business your way. I don't think he'll want anything as extravagant as Father Catamite, just the usual, so long as he can afford it," George said, beckoning Lindsey to follow.

"I cater for all tastes, George. You should bear that in mind," came the reply.

"Here we are then," George said, as he and Lindsey drew near to Ronald's surgery door. George gave it a gentle tap.

"Come in," Ronald shouted.

"Ooh, that sounds familiar!" Lindsey whispered to George, as he pushed open the door.

"Lindsey," Ronald said, a short smile bolting across his lips as he gestured to the chair.

"Ronald, I hardly recognised you with your clothes on!" Lindsey replied.

"Oh, you old bugg ... scoundrel you! How's the old bare-knuckled boxing coming along?" Ronald laughed, giving Lindsey a playful slap.

"Eh?" Lindsey replied, looking at Ronald, then at George, then back to Ronald.

"Will that be all, George, or was there something else?" Ronald queried.

Later that day the gentle meditation of young George was disturbed as Ivor entered the living room and noisily sat down on a sofa opposite him.

"Where's Ronald and the dandy?" Ivor enquired.

"In his surgery," George replied.

"Still? Then it must have been those two I heard arm-wrestling," Ivor mumbled.

"Arm-wrestling?" George asked, his inquisitiveness aroused.

"Well, there's a lot of grunting and groaning going on. I hardly think he's going to have come here to help Ronald move the furniture."

"No, no! Ronald's thinking of buying a toilet from him. He's a salesman. They're probably hammering away at it like there's no tomorrow. I bet if we were flies on the wall in that room, we'd see that Ronald had him over a barrel, even as we speak!" George said, laughing.

"Maybe," Ivor muttered, lifting a newspaper in front of his face so that he no longer had to look at George.

"Anyway, you coming to the fayre tonight?" George asked.

"Fayre?" Ivor said, lowering the newspaper.

"Yes, I heard Nurse Conwy mention it. They've got some stalls and games as well as a Bearded Lady and the like," George said, his eyes widening as though he were a child excitedly speaking of an imminent birthday party. "I'm going to see if Ronald and Lindsey want to come once they've finished."

No sooner had George finished speaking than Ronald and Lindsey entered the room.

"Ah, Doctor Stumpf! We were just talking about you two," George said cheerfully.

"You were? Why? I've not been up to anything," Ronald said furtively, pulling his wig straight.

"Well, Ivor heard you two arm-wrestling and we were wondering how long you were going to be. Ivor and I are thinking of going to the fayre," he explained.

"Arm-wrestling? Oh yes, that's what we were doing," Ronald said.

"So, how do you find old Ronald? He goes hard at it when he wants his pound of flesh, doesn't he? I bet he had you over a barrel alright, eh?" Ivor said, nodding and smiling at Lindsey.

"A table, actually," Lindsay muttered.

"Tell me about this fayre, it sounds really great!" Ronald said, making sure Lindsey was cut off in mid-flow.

"They've got a German band with real Germans and an Italian organ grinder and monkey. They've some trained animals, some stalls, some people who eat real fire! Some puppet shows, alehouses, rides of all sorts, bare-knuckle boxing, as well as a whipping post and stocks," George enthused.

"How delightfully plebeian," Lindsey squealed. "Oh Ronald, do let's go!"

"This is going to be really great - unbelievable. *Nobody* knows more about fayres than me ... tremendous people. Shall we go?" Ronald said, looking around the room. "But what about Nurse Conwy?"

"She's already there," George said. "She's selling something or other."

The four men made their way from the house towards the church, to where the fayre was being held.

"My masters and friend and good people draw near, And look to your purses for that I do say, And though little money in them you do bear, It cost more to get than

to lose in a day," a barker at the fayre was heard to sing as the little troupe drew nearer to the fayre entrance.

"Youth, youth, thou hadst better been starved by the nurse, than live to be hanged for cutting a purse," the song continued.

"Ooh, don't talk to me about cutpurses!" George said as if he were about to impart a pearl or two of wisdom. "I remember in Edinburgh, someone tried to rip open my purse with a sharpened blade attached to his thumb. It was only by a stroke of luck that my scrotum got in the way," he confided, his voice trailing away as the bright colours and sounds began swirling around them.

"What's this then?" Ivor asked George, pausing at the first stall.

"Oh, this is brilliant!" George answered, lifting his arms so that his clenched fists were just a few inches from his chest and shaking them back and forth. "In this game, you pay the man your money and he asks you to think of a number between one and twenty. Then you tell him the number you were thinking of and if it's the same as the number he was thinking of, you get another go!"

"I see," Ivor said. "And what do I win?"

"I just told you! You get another go."

"So, all I win is the chance to think of another number to tell the stallholder, who then tells me whether it was the same as the number he was thinking, right?" Ivor said, folding his arms and looking at Lindsey and nodding in George's direction.

"It's a very popular stall, Ivor," George protested.

"All I can say is that you're easily amused, George," Ivor said sarcastically, moving on.

"Hang on, where's Ronald?" George said, looking around for the absent party.

"Oh, God, he hasn't found the ale tent already, has he?" Ivor said, his face twitching in irritated impatience.

"There won't be any boofing in there, even if he has!" said George. "Hang on, what's that commotion over there, by the whipping post?" he added, pointing at a fracas a little distance away.

"Let's have a look," Ivor said, moving toward the group. "What's going on?" he asked a stallholder as he drew near.

"It's the old man," he said, gesturing at Ronald, who by now was standing in the centre of the crowd. "I told him this wasn't a stall but the whipping post where all those convicted of offences at the fayre were beaten, and he said he didn't care and would give me two shillings if I'd let him flog a few people. I mean, if someone's going to pay me to do my job then I'm not going to be a fool about it, am I?" The man said, his face breaking into a wretched leer, revealing the blackened stumps of what once were teeth. "He even said he'd pay double if they were Mexicans! Sadly, we didn't have any Mexicans but we do have a man that wants to give women the vote! It was all I could do to stop the old fella punching *him* in the face!"

"Good! Sounds like that swine had it coming," Ivor said, turning to George. "Well, George, we can take Ronald with us but I'd rather you than me try and get him away from here! Or we can leave him to his own devices and come back for him later. You choose," Ivor said.

George looked at Ronald, who was already breathing heavily, beads of sweat dripping down his orange face.

"Such stamina!" said Lindsey.

"I think we'll leave him enjoying himself, shall we?" George suggested as the trio moved on.

"Oh look, Ivor, the oddities tent! Can we go in?" George said excitedly, pointing at one particularly drab tent.

"Who wants to see a tent full of liberals!" Ivor replied.

"Ladies and gentlemen, today we have a treat for you. All the way from another country, we have Bushy Babs, the hairiest woman in Wales. By a cruel twist of fate, this unfortunate woman has also been cursed to live a life without breasts, whilst yet another cruel blow has made her womanly parts exactly the same as a man's. Ladies and gentlemen, prepare yourself for the horror that is Bushy Babs," barked the stallholder, whipping the crowds into a state of excitement as he parted them from their cash and ushered them inside. As the lights dimmed and the curtains drew back, Bushy Babs stepped forth.

"Ooh, I say!" said Lindsey.

"That's a man!" someone heckled.

"Don't be so stupid!" Ivor said to the heckler. "You heard what the man said! Do you think these people lie for a living? We're medical men with a scientific brain! Have some sympathy for this poor specimen of womanhood!" Ivor hissed through clenched teeth, smiling as the people in front of him turned around to see who was causing the commotion.

"Next, ladies and gentlemen, we have the most unusual case yet of Siamese twins. What cruel twist of fate created this monster, we can only guess. Born with four legs, four arms, two heads, and two distinct bodies, these Siamese twins have one piece of luck on their side, in that their complete separation from one another has allowed them to lead independent lives. Ladies and gentlemen, I give you Morgan and Jones the barker said.

"This man certainly knows how to get the crowds going," George said enthusiastically.

The curtain drew back to reveal one pale and scrawny man centre stage, sitting on a stool. A minute or so later, a shorter man that looked old enough to be the first man's father ran from the wings.

"Sorry I'm late," the red-faced newcomer said.

"I suppose you'll be telling me next, George, that they're not Siamese twins at all but are just two men who aren't even related stood close to one another!" Ivor scoffed.

"You always exaggerate things, don't you? You think you're so smart! Well, let me tell you, upstairs might be for thinking but downstairs is for dancing," George answered, narrowing his eyes and bringing his face near to Ivor's.

"And what do you mean by that, young man?" Ivor said, drawing himself to the edge of his chair and turning to face his brother.

"Uh ... I don't know!" George answered with venom.

"And now, ladies and gentlemen, the climax of our performance - The Living Head! We can only imagine what it must be like to be born without feet - we can only imagine what it must be like to be born without legs or arms - but what would life be like without a body as well!"

"My dog was born with no nose," shouted a heckler, causing a few titters to ripple around the tent.

"How does he smell?" Ivor queried.

"Horrible!", said the man.

"A bit like Doctor Stumpf then", said George to Ivor.

"Please, ladies and gentlemen. If you're not going to take this very special performance seriously ..." the irritated proprietor said, gesturing for silence.

"Now this should be good!" Ivor said, craning his neck. "Ladies and gentlemen, I give you The Living Head ..."

With that, the curtain rolled back and a large black box was wheeled out, perhaps four feet high and about two feet wide by two feet deep, atop of which was a head.

"That's incredible! In all my years as a Doctor, I've never seen anything like it!" Ivor exclaimed.

"Me neither," George answered, standing to get a better look.

"Now I suppose you're going to tell me there's a man sat inside that box with his head just poking out of a hole!" Ivor scoffed.

"That's it! I'm off to get myself a drink! Are you coming, or not?" George asked.

"Well the show's over, so I might as well," Ivor replied.

"Wait for me, Ducky," Lindsey cooed.

"Lindsey, please! It's Mallard, not Ducky. There is a difference, believe me," Ivor said, drawing Lindsey to one side.

"I hope you remembered to grease your tankard with a piece of herring before you came out," George asked.

"Come out? I haven't come out!" Ronald said, having just joined them "Oh, sorry, I see what you mean, I thought you meant ... oh never mind".

"George, why are you wittering on about greasing tankards with a herring? Are you talking in some code or slang known only to you and other halfwits?" Ivor asked.

"When you have a drink in these places it's always best to make sure you've greased your tankard first, the twisters can't give you a mug full of foam as the beer won't froth," George said, looking rather pleased with himself.

"Oh bollocks, I knew there was something I meant to do before we left. That's your fault for rushing me," Ivor said, kicking George in the backside.

"And watch out when they fill your pipe as they mix coltsfoot with the tobacco as well," George continued.

"George, how do you know so much about these scams?" Ivor enquired, only to see George smiling, keeping his lips firmly shut and nodding his head from side to side. Within a few moments, the trio arrived at the ale tent, where George managed a discreet word with Lindsey.

"I was just saying to Ivor, Lindsey. Watch they don't stuff your pipe full of coltsfoot."

"I beg your pardon!" Lindsey replied, visibly shocked.

"But if you want to grease your tankard with my herring later, don't tell Ivor," George whispered.

"Oh, dear boy, I had no idea! Of course, we can come to some arrangement. But we must be discreet about such things. I should hate to be the *fille de joie* to come between two brothers," Lindsey said, resting a limp hand on George's shoulder.

"Well, I don't want you gulping down mouthfuls of froth, do I?" George added, looking at Lindsey with some confusion.

"Oh, my alabaster Adonis! I'm sure you'd never let me suffer such disappointments," Lindsey added, pursing his lips and narrowing his eyes.

"Doctor Stumpf," George whispered, as Lindsey beckoned a serving girl.

"What is it now, George?" Ronald replied, as though it really were a chore even to speak to the young man.

"That Lindsey. Is he ... is he ... you know ... a bit funny?" George said lowering his voice for the final word.

"What! Of course not! Ha! Funny indeed! He's no more funny than I am," Ronald replied, laughing as he mopped the beads of sweat from his temples.

"That's alright then. It wouldn't worry me - after all, this is practically the nineteenth century, so live and let live, I say - it's just that all that macho posturing of his is getting on my nerves."

"Why George, were you hoping he'd find you attractive? George, let me allay those fears at once – no one finds you attractive," Ivor said, "Especially when you're stood next to people as handsome as Doctor Stumpf and me."

"Yes, they do! Nurse Conwy fancies me," George protested.

"George, Nurse Conwy would fancy anything that could walk upright for more than two consecutive paces without dragging its knuckles on the floor Don't think of it as confirmation of your universal appeal," Ivor said, laughing.

"Right then, four gin and tonics with a dash of lemon – oh, and a length of hose and a funnel," Lindsey said, handing the drinks to his acquaintances. All four suddenly noticed the hush that had descended on the room as every eye trained upon them.

"Bottoms up, boys," Lindsey said, leaning towards George and Ivor. "And up yours, gentlemen!" he added, gesturing to the attendant throng, cheerily raising the glass to his lips as he spoke.

One drink quickly followed another, and all was well until Lindsey started loudly singing a dirty limerick about a young man from Buckley.

"Come on, I think we'd better be off," Ivor said to George.

With that, the little troop arose and left the ale tent.

"Ooh look, an organ grinder," George said, pointing to an elderly Italian cranking the handle of a hurdy-gurdy, whilst a little capuchin monkey banged a wooden bowl and eyed-up the crowd, evidently wondering how his fortunes had fallen so low.

"Isn't that Ronald?" Ivor said, pointing at an orange-faced man walking with singular determination through the crowd towards them. "I thought he was with us but he must have wandered off after we left the tent."

"All that jerking back and fore ... good job I have the best wrists," Ronald said as he approached, rubbing his wrist as he spoke.

"Oh, I gave my wrists a good workout earlier today!" Lindsey said, bursting into paroxysms of laughter and slapping Ronald on the chest.

"Oh look, Ivor, there's some bric-à-brac stalls! Can we go and see what they're selling?" George enthused, leading the gang of four towards the little clutch of stalls set slightly apart from the fun of the fayre.

"Will you look at that! There's a stall selling surgical appliances," Ivor said, his greedy eye scanning the stall for a bargain.

"And will you look at that? There's a medicine chest just like mine!" George said, picking up a mahogany case and opening it so that an array of glass jars filled with coloured powders sparkled in the light. "This is amazing, it even has my initials on it!" George said, shaking his head in disbelief.

"And that cupping set looks just like mine!" Ivor added, sharing George's astonishment at the coincidences.

"Can I help you gentlemen?" came a voice from behind the group as the stallholder returned to the stall.

"Nurse Conwy!" George said, as cheerily as ever.

"No ... I'm ... uh ... Mrs Jones," said the woman nervously.

"This is incredible!" George added. "A stall selling stuff that looks just like ours, run by a woman that looks just like Nurse Conwy."

"I wish Nurse Conwy were here, she'd be amazed!" Ivor added.

"There are more things in heaven and earth, Horatio, than are dreamt of in your philosophy," said Lindsey, froth beginning to form around the edges of his mouth.

"I don't believe this! Ivor, look! I've even found a letter from our father to a man with the same name as me who even lives at our house!" George said, shaking his head in disbelief.

"You buying or looking, 'cause if you're looking you look with your eyes, not your hands," the woman behind the stall barked.

"We've no need to buy a thing from you, my good woman. We have all such sundries as your tawdry stall purveys in our copiously furnished surgery," Ivor said haughtily, drawing his coat around him theatrically and tossing his head, then turning and falling to the ground, having lost his footing in the overflow seeping from the gentleman's latrine.

"Come and see the genuine Blackbeard, Terror of the Seven Seas," barked a particularly unpleasant-looking hawker.

"Oh, can we, Ivor?" George said, dashing to the tent.

"Lead the way," Ivor said.

"Is it the real Blackbeard?" George asked, trying to peer inside the tent.

"The one and only," replied the man, quickly selling George a ticket.

"This is great!" George said excitedly as Ivor, Lindsay, and Ronald sat beside him.

As the bedraggled audience quieted themselves, the curtains drew back. A lithe young sailor jumped onto the stage and began dancing the Sailor's Hornpipe.

"Yoo-hoo!" Lindsey shouted, standing and waving excitedly.

"Get him back in his seat," Ivor hissed to George, who obeyed Ivor's command and pulled the back of Lindsey's coat so that he fell back into his seat.

"Ladies and gentlemen," said the sailor, having finished his merry dance. "Here he is, the saltiest seaman of them all! Blackbeard!"

With that, an overweight, sweating mound appeared from the wings.

"Thank you for coming," said Blackbeard, strapping on an accordion. "I'd like to sing you a little song. It's called *I May Be a Monocled Monoped, But I'm More of a Man Than Most* and goes like this," he said, launching into his song.

"Well, I don't think this is very frightening," Ivor said to George disappointedly.

"I do, Ivor - that's Eldritch's brother! Don't you recognise the fat fugger? I'd have never cut his leg off if I'd known he was Blackbeard!" George quaked.

"Eh?" Ivor grunted, quizzically training his eyes upon the young sailor on stage as he mimed the picking of weevils from biscuits into his routine.

"The man whose leg I cut off! The one who came back from the grave!" George stammered, clutching Ivor's coat with a look of terror on his face.

"Uh!" Ivor gasped, taking a sharp intake of breath and looking at George with the same expression of horror as George.

"And what's worse, I recognise the other one as well. He's the one Ronald took the whip to in the surgery when he came to see me about his scurvy," George said, his teeth chattering.

"Oh, God, we're done for now! This is all your fault for wanting to come into this stupid tent in the first place," Ivor said, turning his head towards George in accusation.

"Oh, that's it, shoot the messenger why don't you!" George answered, folding his arms and reclining in his seat.

"Look, George, this isn't the time to sulk. We have to use all our stealth and cunning to get out of here," Ivor said, his brow creasing and his eyes bobbing around like apples in a barrel.

"And now, Seaman Staines and I would like to sing that old family favourite – *On the Good Ship Venus*," said Blackbeard, his first song having whipped the audience into a state of apathy.

"Oh, now I like this one," George said, making himself comfortable.

"George, we've got to go! I don't think you realise how perilous our position is sitting here," Ivor hissed, bringing his head close to George's.

"Ivor, I don't like to be the one to break this to you, but it just got worse," said George.

"Eh? What are you talking about now?" Ivor asked, confusedly.

"Cast your eyes stagewards," George continued

"Oh, I don't believe this!" Ivor said, burying his face in his hands.

"He's an old hoofer though, isn't he! A real old pro!" George said as he watched Lindsey, up on stage, attempting to dance the Sailor's Hornpipe along with the tune. With his arms pressed tightly to his side and his legs lashing out at all angles, his performance only stopped when he fell from the stage and knocked himself out.

"That's just marvellous, isn't it! It means we have to sit through all of this now. We can't just leave him here, which means we've got to stay," Ivor said with unhappy resignation. "Wait! Ask Ronald if he's got his whip with him! At least then we'll have a fighting chance if things turn ugly," he added as he clutched George's arm, his face pale with desperation.

George leant over to Ronald and whispered a few things in his ear. There followed a prolonged discussion, in which George related the entire story. Finally, the discussion over, Ivor looked over to Ronald, who nodded an assured affirmation and tapped the palm of his hand against his breast pocket.

"Well?" Ivor asked, as George finished speaking and returned to his seat.

"Well, what?" George said with a look of dazed bewilderment on his face.

"Has he got his horsewhip with him?" Ivor asked, raising his hands to bring them tightly around George's throat before checking himself.

"No," George replied.

"No! Well, that's that then. We're shafted now, aren't we!" Ivor said, the colour draining from his cheeks to such a degree that he turned a shade of what can only be called *underside of trout*.

Finally, the show drew to a close and the audience left, leaving the three Doctors, Lindsey, the two sailors and the show's hawker.

"Now we're for it!" Ivor said, trying to whisper to George from the side of his mouth.

"You!" Eldritch's brother shouted from the stage.

"He's spotted you!" Ivor said.

"Erm ... sorry!" George said, shrinking into his seat as the huge figure approached.

"Sorry? No need to be sorry! You did me a real favour! I'd had enough of fuggin' around. I've never had so much money! I'm in a new career completely. I hire myself out for parties as a pirate. The women love it! I go there, sing a few shanties, dance a few jigs, tell them all that they might think I've got one-and-a- half legs but I've only got one 'cause the other's not a leg at all - know what I mean!" he leered, nudging Ivor in the ribs with his elbow.

"And I did bring you back from the dead?" George offered in his defence.

"Dead, my arse! I was drunk, that was all," Eldritch said, turning to his compadre.

"Well, we know that's a lie for a start," George said to Ivor as surreptitiously as he could manage.

"Jonesy - sorry, Seaman Staines - come and meet some friends of mine!" bellowed Blackbeard.

"Ahoy there, maties!" said Seaman Staines, bounding around with all the vitality of youth. "You!" he said, suddenly stopping and pointing at Ronald. "And you!" he continued, pointing at George.

"It was him, not me!" George said, pointing at Ronald, raising his arm in front of his face to protect himself from the expected blows.

"No! No! I want to thank you two. That beating you gave me was the best thing that ever happened to me. A damn good thrashing flayed some sense into me. Scurvy? Pah, I've had worse," he snorted.

"I remember a time when men were proud to get scurvy and lose a limb or two," said Ronald looking from Seaman Staines to Blackbeard. "It was a sign they'd become a man if they had cholera or the plague. Nowadays they have a little bit of syphilis and they're running to the Doctor as if it's the end of the world! I remember a time when I was young and so crippled with bone spurs that I could barely play a round of golf - my father cured them with his belt!

And do you know what? I thanked him for it! A good thrashing is all these so-called sick need with their pre-existing health conditions! Never mind all this namby-pamby mumbo-jumbo! Get a rod to their back and beat the devils out, that's my motto," said Ronald, proudly reclining in his seat.

"Bloody liar, his father was a millionaire," Ivor whispered to George from the side of his mouth.

"Oh, but Ivor, I almost forgot! What about Lindsey?" George said suddenly remembering their unconscious friend.

"Oh, bugger! You're right. I'd forgotten about him. Sorry gentlemen, the man that got up on stage with you earlier was a friend of ours. He'd had a little too much to drink, I think, and became quite excited when he saw the sailor dancing about," Ivor explained.

"He's not looking good, Ivor," George shouted, having already moved to the front of the stage.

"No, he isn't," said Ivor, as he and Ronald drew alongside.

"Do you think we ought to call a Doctor?" George asked.

"George, we are Doctors!" Ivor said, looking at Ronald with a wry smile and nodding in George's direction, quickly losing his smile as Ronald grimaced back.

"Oh, if only Nurse Conwy were here!" George said, wringing his hands.

"Why?" Ivor asked.

"She'd be able to look at our appointments and tell us whether we're busy or not," George replied.

"I could probably fit him in Tuesday week," Ronald said.

"If he's really ill I could probably make an emergency call," Ivor added.

"Oh, this is ridiculous, let's carry him back to the surgery and have a look at the book to find out how busy we are," George said.

"George, I'm proud of you! That's the first good idea you've had all day," Ivor said, patting George on the back. "Right then Ronald, you grab his legs and I'll grab his arms," he added, pointing Ronald towards Lindsey's feet, lest he'd forgotten where they were.

"See you, fellas," Ivor said to the two sailors as he staggered to the tent exit. "Loved the act! Very professional! Break a leg now!" he added, as Blackbeard saw the joke and playfully pretended to shoot them.

"Oh Ivor, look! They've some children fighting! Can I have a bet please?" George wailed, rushing towards the roped ring where a rum-looking villain was taking a few bets on the next bout.

"Well, we're going to take Lindsey back to the house. Don't be long, you hear," Ivor said, allowing George his last frisson.

Back at the house, Ivor and Ronald dropped Lindsey onto the couch.

"Phew! He was a weight, wasn't he!" Ronald said, taking a handkerchief from his pocket and mopping his brow.

"Perhaps you should have had him on your back instead," Ivor suggested.

"What! What are you insinuating? I've never had a man on my back in my life. Oh sorry, I thought you meant ... oh, it doesn't matter what I thought. Look, here's George! Hello George!" Ronald said, rushing to take him by the hand.

"Eh?" George grunted, looking at Ronald and then at Ivor, who shrugged his shoulders indicating he didn't understand either.

"Did you win?" Ivor asked cheerily.

"No, it was fixed!" George moaned, flopping into a chair. "I thought I had a dead cert until Tiny Tom started using his crutches. From there on in, the game wasover."

"Oh well, never mind," Ivor replied.

"How's Lindsey?" George inquired.

"That's right, I knew there was something we had to do! Nurse Conwy! Nurse Conwy!" Ivor shouted.

"Yes," Nurse Conwy said flatly, opening the door to her door and standing silhouetted against the red glow of her room, the wind billowing through the open window going some way to mask her breathlessness.

"Have you been running?" Ivor asked.

"No! Was that all you wanted?" Nurse Conwy hissed.

"No. Can we see Lindsey? Do you know?" Ivor asked.

"What? There he is, on the sofa," Nurse Conwy replied pointing at the prone figure of Lindsey curled up on the sofa.

"Yes, I know where he is, but can we see him?" Ivor explained.

"What Ivor's trying to say is, do you know whether we're busy or not?" Ronald added.

"Are you going to perform another miracle Doctor Stumpf? You remind me more of Jesus every day!" Nurse Conwy said.

"You're not the first person to have said that, Nurse Conwy, but I'm actually *better* than Jesus as I'm British! I also charge for my miracles whereas Jesus did it for nothing! Think of the profit he could have made feeding the four-hundred thousand! Yes, *nobody* reads the Bible more than me!" Doctor Stumpf explained.

"Nelly, this is costing me money what with you charging by the hour," came a voice from within Nurse Conwy's room.

"Uh, sorry, I have to go," Nurse Conwy said hurriedly.

"What was that? Have you got a man in there? I don't pay you good money to have men in your room!" Ivor said, trying to follow Nurse Conwy.

"Are you surveilling me?" she asked. "First it was the oven and now it's you!" she added as she slammed the door in his face.

"Incredible!" Ivor said, turning back. "And what are you looking so glum about?" he asked George.

"I thought she fancied me," he answered miserably.

"George, I've said it once and I'll say it again! No one fancies you."

"I've had enough of this. I need a drink," George said, quickly standing up and moving towards the drinks cabinet.

"Our faces might very well be like Dick's, George, but you'll never be as attractive as me! Didn't you see those Romanies there tonight with their swarthy good looks? I could tell they were wondering whether I was one of them," Ivor said smugly.

"You're not wrong there. Most people think you're one of them," Ronald slurred.

I'll Have a Kiss Behind the Cowshed

George opened the drinks cabinet and perused the array of drinks inside, making a mental note of which drinks he could use for his favourite cocktails.

"Right then, who's for a *Quickie*?"

"No, George! I absolutely forbid it!" Ivor said sternly.

"A *Quickie*?" Ronald asked, his curiosity aroused.

"Yes, it's one of my cocktails," George said, making growling noises and shaking his head from side to side.

"Oh, it's a drink, is it? Boring!" Ronald said, despairing at the anti-climax.

"George, you're not to make one. I forbid it," Ivor said sternly as George took a pair of pint pots from the drinks cabinets and reached for a bottle of whiskey.

"Oh, shush!" said George.

"George, put that whiskey down! I don't want you touching that!" Ivor said, trying to enforce his threats with a pointed finger. George, ignoring Ivor's disapproval, continued unabated.

"George, you're not to pick up that liniment rub. I won't allow it!" Ivor said.

"How do you like your lemons?" George asked Ronald.

"What are you implying?" Ronald said furtively.

"George, you're not to put that in that drink," Ivor demanded.

"Here you are, then," George said, as he picked up the drinks and walked toward Ronald.

"George, I don't want you drinking that drink! Remember what happened last time?" Ivor said.

"Down the hatch!" George said, clinking glasses with Ronald.

"A cheeky little number," George commented, turning red and breaking into a sweat. "But with a really earthy nutty, flavour that lingers long after the drink has gone, reminding one of those long summer days!" he added, his eyes rolling back so far into his skull that only the whites remained visible.

"I don't have my funnel with me," Ronald said.

"Oh, okay," George said, loosening his clothing.

"Unbelievable! Of all the stupid things to do! I can't believe it! My own brother! And Ronald – don't even think about it! You ought to have more sense, a man of your age," Ivor said, throwing himself into the back of his chair and drawing the corners of his mouth down, looking around the room in disgust.

I'll Have a Kiss Behind the Cowshed

"Don't you preach to me! I may be having a little company later and I want to be relaxed. I want to make sure I'm at my most charming!" Ronald said.

"I thought everybody loved you!" Ivor said, laughing, but the barb was ignored as Doctor Stumpf retired to his room, pulling a length of hose from his pocket as he left.

"Do you fancy another one, Doctor Stumpf?" George shouted, struggling to stand.

A few minutes later, Doctor Stumpf returned taking tiny steps and clenching his buttocks. He opened his mouth only to find that, for a moment, he'd forgotten how to speak.

"I said, do you fancy another one, Doctor Stumpf?" George asked.

"Covfefe. Get me a covfefe," Ronald slurred.

"Has Ronald been boofing, Ivor? No wonder he can say that alcohol never passes his lips! He can't even say coffee," George whispered to Ivor.

"That's Doctor Stumpf to you! He pays the wages, don't forget," Ivor admonished.

"Okay, party-pooper! Would you like a cocktail … to drink!" George countered.

"No, I would … well, maybe just a small one! You know what I'm like when I've had too much to drink!" Ivor said, shaking his head as though he were letting long tresses fall free.

114

"Right then, three *Quickies* it is," George said, staggering back towards the drink cabinet.

"I'm a fool to myself! I just know I'm going to regret this in the morning," Ivor said excitedly.

"Ivor, have we got any soap?" George said, turning to Ivor and squinting as he tried to focus.

"Oh, don't tell me we've no clean glasses!" Ivor said in annoyed disappointment.

"No! No! Plenty of clean glasses. I just wanted to froth up the drinks a bit, you know? Give them a bit of a head," George slurred.

"Oh, don't worry about that. I'm sure they'll be fine," Ivor added.

"Well, if you say so. I don't want you to think I've sacrificed quality in my haste," George added, turning back to the cabinet and mixing the drinks with aplomb. "Here we are then," George said, returning with a tray of drinks.

"It's been a long time since I had one of ..." Ivor said, bringing the glass to his mouth and taking a long slurp.

"I feel warm all over. It's as if I'm wrapped up in warm feathers," Ronald said, suddenly opening his eyes. "Did I just say that out loud?"

"Ivor, you alright?" George asked, looking at Ivor, who was sitting completely immobile staring ahead with unblinking eyes and a frozen expression.

I'll Have a Kiss Behind the Cowshed

"I never remember it being like this!" Ivor confessed. "The last time I felt like this was that time I accidentally injected myself when practising involuntary euthanasia on Dangleberry Jones."

"Is he still around?" Ronald asked.

"Not any more!" Ivor smirked. "He'll rue the day he ever tried not paying Doctor Ivor Mallard!"

"Do you know, Ivor? You're my best mate, you are!" George said, resting a hand on Ivor's shoulder.

"Thanks, George. I'm very fond of you too," Ivor said, looking a little embarrassed.

"No, but you're my *best* mate!" George emphasised.

"I know, George, you just said," Ivor replied, frowning and laughing at the same time.

"Eh, you know me! Is my name George or what?" George asked.

"Yes, it is George. That's why I call you George," Ivor said slowly, emphasising each word.

"Are you making fun of me?" George slurred. "Don't try and make me look stupid, 'cause I'll do you any day of the week," George said, trying to stand and beckoning Ivor towards him with both hands.

"I really don't think you need me to make you look stupid!" Ivor said sarcastically. George looked to Ronald and then back to Ivor in strange, jerky movements.

"Don't get funny with me, pal! I could have you any time! You say the time and the place and I'll be there," George said, rolling up his shirt sleeves.

"Leave it, George, he's not worth it," Ronald slurred.

"George, sit down," Ivor insisted

"Oh, that's it! Soon back down when you see a bit of muscle, don't you?" George scoffed.

"George, I don't want to fight with you. You started it!" Ivor said.

"I started it? Me!" said George, drawing back his arm and closing one eye to aim, as if he were about to fire an arrow. "I'm gonna get you for that."

George lunged forward with all his force, missing Ivor completely and sending himself into a spin, culminating in his falling to the floor in a tangle of limbs.

"There, feel better now?" Ivor asked, moving towards the drinks cabinet for another *Quickie*.

"I'm sorry Ivor!" George sobbed. "I really, really love you! You're my best mate, you are. I know women find me attractive but that's because I'm young. You're just handsome you are, Ivor," George said as he crawled across the floor on all fours, crying.

"If you can't beat 'em, join 'em," Ivor mumbled and took a large swig of his drink. No sooner had the last drop been quaffed than his knees buckled and he fell to the floor in a sweating heap.

"I love you, George," Ivor said, trying to stop the room spinning above his glazed eyes. "You've always been like a brother to me."

George and Ivor burst out laughing and hugged each other, each using the other to try and get themselves upright.

"If only Lindsey weren't unconscious," said George, as he flopped into a seat next to the comatose dandy. "He'd teach us a thing or two, wouldn't he!"

"You're not joking there," Ivor added

"Hey Ivor, is he a bit of a hard case? He's pretty keen on all that machismo stuff, isn't he?" George asked.

"Well, he gave me twenty per cent off that toilet I ordered when I told him you were a bare-knuckle champion and wanted to give him a leathering," Ivor laughed, stuffing his pipe with something 'medicinal'.

"You what?" George said, temporarily sobering.

"I told him you'd give him a good seeing to unless I got the toilet I ordered cheaper," Ivor confessed.

"You swine! How dare you!" George said, trying to shake some sobriety into his befuddled head.

"Oh, grow up! You wanted an inside toilet, didn't you? You were the one always moaning about your arse sticking to the rim on the outside one in winter. Well, now we've got a nice indoor one! All you have to do is say that you're in training if he asks," Ivor advised dismissively.

"I can't believe you said that about me! Me? Your own brother! Wouldn't it have been easier for you to ask him for a fight, or an arm wrestle, for a discount?" George queried.

"Oh, I tried that first, believe me!" Ivor said earnestly.

"And?" George demanded.

"The bugger beat me!" Ivor said quietly.

"He beat you!" George exclaimed as Ronald began laughing.

"He's stronger than he looks!" Ivor remonstrated.

Suddenly, there was a quiet tap at the door.

"That'll be my lady friend," Ronald said, his face glowing like an orange ember. He made his way to the door and after some difficulty in remembering how doors worked, managed to swing it open. There, in the light from the room, stood Bushy Babs, the bearded lady who they'd seen at the fayre.

Remembering their manners, Ivor and George managed to stand as the woman entered the room.

"I'm George, you must be Bushy Babs," George said, extending a hand of greeting that was already shaking from the effects of the alcohol.

"No, that's my stage name. My real name is Clive ... uh ... Clivella, I mean," came the gravelly reply.

"Clivella, that's a pretty name," said Ivor. "Is it French?"

"*Oui, Monsieur,*" Clivella replied.

"That's really great – unbelievable. *Nobody* knows more about bearded ladies than me ... tremendous people. Please, my dear, take a seat. Your little poppet shan't be a moment," Ronald said, skipping as lightly as clenched buttocks and his bulky frame could manage, across the room, and over to George.

"Get us a drink, and make it one that doesn't burn! I couldn't sit down for days last time!" said Ronald, squirming at the memory.

"Well Clivella, we're all having a little drink. Would you care to join us?" George asked.

"Please," said Clivella, nervously toying with her Adam's apple. George finished mixing the drink and turned to walk towards Ronald and Clivella, who were now sitting next to one another on the sofa. Ronald nibbled at Clivella's ear, winding his tongue around a particularly coarse tuft of beard. Almost before he knew it, the hairs had wound tightly around his dentures and as Clivella reached forward to take her drink, Ronald's dentures were torn from his mouth and plopped into Clivella's lap.

"You seem to have ... uh ... dropped something," Clivella said, picking up the teeth as large trails of saliva sought freedom now that they had the opportunity to escape.

"Oh, God, sorry!" Ronald said, his face looking as if a workforce of tiny miners who'd been excavating the inside of his head had just experienced a major cave-in.

"I say, old Ronald is going for it," George said, returning to his seat and almost sitting on Ivor."Look at him now!" George exclaimed.

As the two Quacks looked over, Ronald was unbuttoning his shirt, revealing a flabby pair of pectorals and a stomach that resembled last week's balloons, if balloons came in the colour of burnt tangerines.

"So, gentlemen, did you see the show tonight?" Clivella asked George and Ivor, as Ronald continued his attempts at foreplay.

"We did! And very good it was too," Ivor slurred.

"We couldn't believe The Living Head could we, Ivor? As scientific medical men, we know a thing or two about the human body ...," said George.

"I should say!" Ivor interrupted

121

"But we've never seen anything like that. I mean, where's his arse?" George asked.

"Oh really, George! Not in front of a lady!" said Ivor disapprovingly. "You'll have to excuse my brother. He's the uncouth one in the family. Actually, we're both a pair of nobs! Show Clivella your little Dick Uppham, George," Ivor encouraged.

Clivella looked surprised but managed a smile as she took a sip of her drink.

"Not now, Ivor, I'm too drunk," George said. "I hope you don't mind us prying," he continued.

"No, that's quite alright. People often ask questions. A lot of people don't believe I'm a woman and ask if I'm a man," Clivella said, laughing.

"Now that's ridiculous!" George scoffed.

"Ooh!" came a groan from the far side of the sofa as Lindsey stirred.

"Lindsey's back in the land of the living!" George said.

"Thanks to us!" Ivor added. "If it hadn't been for our medical care, who knows what could have happened!"

"Oh, my head hurts. Where am I?" Lindsey said, sitting upright and rubbing his temple.

"You fell off the stage when you were dancing with that sailor, remember?" Ivor offered.

"What!" Lindsey said, standing upright and walking towards Ivor with a swagger.

"I don't know about you, Ivor, and I can't put my finger on it but he seems a bit different. Do you think that bang on the head has done something to him?" George said quietly, looking at the floor as he did so.

"Oh, I say, I love the frock!" Lindsey said, his attention having been drawn from Ivor towards Clivella.

"Would you like a drink, Lindsey?" George offered, standing as he spoke.

"Bloody right I would. Got any snuff as well? I reckon I could snort a lungful!" Lindsey said, jumping towards George, shadowboxing as he moved.

George handed Lindsey his drink and returned to where he had been sitting, next to Ivor.

"I've got it!" George whispered.

"Have you? Well, don't come and sit next to me! It might be catching!" Ivor said, shifting uneasily in his seat.

"No, about Lindsey. The difference, remember?" George explained.

"Oh yes! What? I must confess, he seems a little different to me as well," Ivor said thoughtfully.

"Maybe. I think it's the snuff," George said.

"You're right! Oh, God, why do these things always happen to us? Everywhere I go I seem to be surrounded by sick people!" Ivor said, wringing his hands in despair.

"Hey! What are you pair of turds whispering about?" Lindsey shouted, watching - with a mixture of amusement and disgust - Ronald's flabby torso wobbling and shuddering in lust.

A huge bang suddenly came from Nurse Conwy's room, as the door was flung open to reveal who her customer had been: Eldritch!

"You! I want a word with you!" Eldritch said, grabbing hold of George by the throat.

"Eldritch, I thought you were dead!" George gasped.

"Hoped, you mean! No, I've been pleasuring the lovely Nelly with my company. A Ploughman's Lunch and every 'orrible thing you fancy for tuppence," Eldritch said, his fat fingers digging into George's neck.

"Tuppence? That's very reasonable"! George gasped.

"Go on, George! I can tell by the look in his eyes that he's running scared," Ivor enthused from a safe distance.

"Leave the boy alone!" came a voice implacable and chilling.

"Eh?" grunted Eldritch, loosening his grip on George who fell to the floor gasping for breath.

"You heard me, fatty. I said leave the boy alone!" Lindsey said, his eyes narrowing, a cheroot smouldering between his lips.

"Why, do you fancy some?" Eldritch said, lunging towards Lindsey with his arms outstretched.

As he did so, Lindsey brought both arms up swiftly in a praying motion, parting Eldritch's arms in one deft move. Then, knocking Eldritch's right forearm with his left, he launched a powerful right hook into his face.

Before Eldritch had time to respond, Lindsey grabbed a hold of Eldritch's left arm and, using his massive weight, spun him like a top towards a window. It was all too unexpected for Eldritch and he could do nothing to save himself from plummeting from the window and onto the road below.

"Well, that's just marvellous, isn't it?" said Ivor, running to the window and peering into the street below. "For the second time in twelve hours, we've got Eldritch's dead body to get rid of. This man has more bloody lives than a cat!" He added, running his hands through his white hair.

"Ah well! All that throttling has put me in a party mood," said George, rubbing his hands together. "Lindsey, do you fancy a *Quickie*?"

"What sort of man do you think I am?" said Lindsey, giving George a slap with the back of his hand.

"What was that for? I was only offering you a drink," George protested.

"He was, you know. I distinctly heard him," Ivor added. "A *Quickie* is a drink. Same as a *Kiss Behind the Cowshed*, only with laudanum instead of gin to give it that bit of ...."

"*Je ne sais quoi*," George offered.

"Exactly! I knew the Germans would have a phrase for it," Ivor said.

"It's all that Sangria they drink," George added, making his way to the drinks cabinet where he began making a large punch bowl of drink. Ivor alternated between looking at the large splat made by Eldritch underneath the window and frowning. Lindsey swaggered around the room, belching and scratching. whilst Ronald's seduction continued unabated.

"I love your hairs," Ronald whispered, running his fingers along Clivella's forearm. "They're so soft!"

"Oh, Ronald," said Clivella, playfully grabbing Ronald's nose and giving it such a hard tweak that Ronald's eyes watered.

"Please don't change! I always want to remember you as you are now, here with me," Ronald said. "Here, together, the moonbeams catching the flecks in your bush," he continued, hoping his words were hypnotising Clivella into a trance.

"I won't!" said Clivella. "I want to remember you too, as you are now, the soft glow of the candlelight on your tangerine cheeks, the gentle twinkling of the candelabra upon your toupee, the moonlight shimmering on your dentures ..." Clivella said, closing her eyes and taking a large swig of her drink.

"Right, here we are!" George said, returning with a full punchbowl. "Who's up for a *Quickie*?" he asked, snorting like a naughty schoolboy.

"Ronald's hoping," Ivor mumbled.

"Lindsey, do you want a *Kiss Behind the Cowshed* or would you rather have a *Quickie*?"

Lindsey took a step back in astonishment, looking around the room as though he could hardly believe what he was hearing.

"You what?" Lindsey began, his lip curling in astonishment for a moment, just before leaping toward George and chasing him maniacally around the room.

"I can give you a *Knee Trembler* if you'd prefer?" George offered, as he ran in frantic circles around the last piece of furniture they possessed, but the attempt at placating Lindsey fell on deaf ears.

"Come on, Ronald, do something!" Ivor said helplessly.

"Stand aside," Ronald said, pushing Ivor out of the way and standing in the place he had vacated.

"What are you going to do?" Ivor asked.

"It's an old trick my father showed me," Ronald said, taking his teeth from his mouth and swinging them in his arm as though he were bowling in a game of cricket. Suddenly, without warning, the teeth spun from his hand and hit Lindsey straight between the eyes, knocking him out cold.

"Hooray!" George applauded. "That was just like David and Goliath! Only Lindsey's smaller than you ... and you used your teeth and not a rock."

"And Goliath hadn't just been asked if he fancied a *Knee Trembler*," Ivor observed.

"Good point," George conceded. "Anyway, I hardly like to ask, but who would like a drink?"

Drink followed drink followed drink.

"Are you alright, sweetest?" asked Ronald, concerned that Clivella didn't seem to be enjoying herself. "I was hoping a few drinks might loosen your draw ... tongue, sorry, and we might talk until our little hearts beat as one."

"I *am* drinking. I'm just a girl who can hold her liquor," Clivella said coyly, causing both George and

Ivor to snigger, both of them now crawling around on the floor.

"Have some of this, man," Ivor said, handing George a clay pipe full of sweet-smelling herbs from Lebanon. "It'll blow your stockings off!"

"Hey, Lindsey! Lindsey!" George said, poking Lindsey in the ribs.

"Leave it, George, he's not worth it," Ivor mumbled.

"No! Lindsey," George said, dismissing Ivor's suggestion and continuing to poke Lindsey as hard as he could. "Lindsey, man, have a suck on this."

"As the actress said to the bishop!" Ivor said, bursting into high-pitched laughter.

Slowly Lindsey came to and took a large toke on Ivor's clay pipe.

"I've gone numb all over," he said, blinking and trying to focus.

"I know. Great, isn't it!" George said. "Do you want some Doctor Stumpf?"

"No! The Devil's Lettuce isn't for me!" Ronald shouted.

"George, go and get us some biscuits, will you? I'm starving!" Ivor slurred.

"God, Ivor, I could murder some food!" George dribbled.

"I'll go!" Clivella said, jumping from her seat. "Where is the kitchen?"

"Over there somewhere," Ivor said, drawing himself up onto his elbow, his eyes a fearful blood red.

"Now, won't you have a *cocktail*, Lindsey?" George asked, emphasising the fact that he had changed the offending term.

"Yes, go on then," Lindsey said, picking up the dentures that had knocked him out and looking at them with some confusion before realising what they were.

"She's been gone a long time, hasn't she?" Ivor asked, referring to Clivella.

"Are you drunk?" came a voice Ivor hadn't expected to hear, causing him to open puffy red eyes and focus.

"Oh, it's you, Nurse Conwy. I thought it was a woman come in here for a moment," Ivor slurred.

"Answer me! Are you drunk?" Nurse Conwy repeated.

"I should bloody well hope so! I've drunk enough," Ivor answered in irritation, causing George and Lindsey to let out a few giggles and Ronald to let out a snore. "Doesn't look like Ronald will be getting any tonight then!" Ivor said, turning his head jerkily, closing and opening his eyes with exaggerated movements as he spoke.

"No, but I know a very, very naughty boy who will," Nurse Conwy said seductively, taking Ivor by the hand and leading him to her room.

God, My Head Hurts!

"Oh, God, my head hurts!" George said, lifting his head from the floor for an instant, then letting it return and screwing up his eyes. "My eyes feel as though there's somebody behind them trying to lever them out with a spoon."

"My God, what was in that drink last night?" Lindsey said, raising his hands to his temples and pressing them so hard his knuckles went white.

George sought to move himself, but the effort was too much for him and he collapsed in a heap, pressing his eyes in a vain attempt to make them feel they were in back their correct orbits.

"I only wanted a few drinks at the fayre," he explained. "Where did it all go wrong?"

"Oh, don't mention drinks! I think I'm going to be sick!" Lindsey said, rolling from the sofa and crawling to the window from which Eldritch had hurtled the night before.

George managed to sit upright and began rubbing the back of his neck, carefully opening his eyes.

"Doctor Stumpf, wake up!" George said, spying the old Doctor, saliva dripping from his toothless mouth in huge drools, his flabby breasts visible through his open shirt, resting like two slices of squashed orange tripe upon one another.

"Where's Bushy Babs gone?" Lindsey said, taking a huge gulp of fresh air from the open window before turning back into the room to confront the odours of chemicals, alcohol, sweat and flatulence.

"Never mind the lovely Clivella, where's the furniture gone!" George said, opening his eyes wide as he suddenly realised that all that was left in the room were the two sofas upon which Ronald and Lindsey had lain.

"And our clothes!" Lindsey said, looking down at himself clad in nothing but his drawers.

"And where's Ivor? He's can't have been stolen as well?" George said, looking under the sofas.

"Help!" came a whimpering voice from Nurse Conwy's room.

"Did you just hear something?" George said nervously.

"Leave me alone. I'm trying to stop myself feeling sick!" Lindsey answered dismissively, placing his head on the windowsill and letting out an agonised groan.

"Help!"

"There it was again!" George said, clambering to his feet. Nervously, he made his way to Nurse Conwy's door and pressed the side of his head against its dark panelling.

"Help!" came the voice, soft and desperate.

George gave the handle a careful twist and peered through the gap. There, in front of him, was Ivor, shackled and chained to Nurse Conwy's bed.

"Well, well, well, what have we here?" George said, letting the door swing open.

"Look, George, it's not what you think!" Ivor said, struggling against his bondage.

"Who's been a naughty boy, then?" George said, walking into the room.

"I can't remember what happened, George. It's your fault! If you hadn't been giving everyone a *Quickie* this would never have happened."

"Oh, so it's my fault, is it?" George asked, bemusedly.

"Of course! If you hadn't been so busy having a *Quickie*, you'd have been able to have kept an eye on me. You know what I'm like when I'm drunk. I can't believe I had that drink at the fayre in the first place! That was the start of this whole debacle," Ivor said, retching as he thought of the gin he had quaffed at the fayre the previous night and how it had precipitated the mess in which he now found himself.

"Ivor, why are these sheets so wet?" George asked, patting the sheets on which Ivor lay. Ivor smiled back sheepishly.

"And where did that donkey come from!" George continued, suddenly spying the animal resting in the corner of the room after the rigours of the night.

"Oh look, George, can you just untie me!" Ivor barked

"I don't know about that now!" George said, shaking his head as if he really wanted to untie Ivor but to do so would be more than his job was worth. "Doctor Stumpf, Lindsey! Come and look at this! Ivor's been a naughty boy!"

"George, you swine! I'll get you for this," Ivor helplessly hissed as Lindsey staggered to the open door, quickly followed by Ronald.

"So, where's the lovely Nelly?" Lindsey asked.

"Ivor kissed her and she turned into an ass," George said, pointing to the corner of the room and the indignant-looking donkey.

"Look, we're not at some sordid peep show you know! Why don't you just wheel me down to the fayre and charge the punters a penny each to come and have a gawp? You obviously think the spectacle is good entertainment!" Ivor hissed, again straining at the chains that bound him, but to no avail.

"I know one thing," Ronald observed. "He'll never be nicknamed *Ivor Whopper*!"

"Alright, so I slept with Nurse Conwy! Are you happy now? Yes, I was drunk and yes, she charged me fourpence ... and I didn't even get a Ploughman's Lunch thrown in!" Ivor said wistfully. "Now, the joke's over, can you please untie me?"

With the distraction quickly losing its appeal, George's head began to thump again in the same discordant manner as the German oompah band that had tyrannised the fayre the previous evening. Now, the thought of all those huge bearded Germans in their tight leather shorts made his stomach turn and he too began to feel sick.

"Anyway Ivor, just to start the day with a smile, I thought I'd tell you that Nurse Conwy's disappeared," George said, struggling with Ivor's shackles.

"Well, that's one bit of good news!" Ivor squirmed.

"Trouble is, so has all the furniture and Clivella," George said, looking at Ronald.

"Oh, balls!" Ronald shouted, stamping his foot and returning to his seat, whereupon he folded his arms and sank into a moody sulk, evidently only just realising Clivella had gone.

"All the furniture?" Ivor asked.

"Well, not all the furniture! We've two sofas left," George joked.

"Where's it all gone? Who's taken it, for Christ's sake?" Ivor asked.

"I don't know. That's what's puzzling me," George answered. "Look, Ivor, this is no good. It's padlocked! I need a key. Hang on, what's this?" George said, reaching out for a letter beneath Ivor's pillow.

"What is it?" Ivor asked

"It says 'Mallard, I left the keys where I usually leave your change - Nelly," George read aloud. "Right then, Ivor, where's that?   On the mantelpiece?"

"Er, not quite, George," Ivor said blushing. "In fact, I think it would be better if you got some bolt cutters."

"Don't be daft, just tell me where the keys are and I'll have you out in a jiffy," George said, scanning the room.

"George, just get some bolt cutters please," Ivor implored.

"But the keys …."

"George! If you go to my room, you'll find some bolt cutters I stashed away just in case something like this ever came up. They're under the squeaky floorboard.

George shrugged his shoulders and did as he was bid, returning a minute or so later with the bolt cutters.

"There you go!" George said as the last of the chains were cut.

"Thank God for that!" Ivor said, jumping to his feet. A large bunch of keys fell to the floor as he did so.

"Look, they were here all the time!" George said, stooping to pick them up as Ivor quickly kicked them to one side.

"We don't need them now, do we?" Ivor reasoned, taking a sheet from the bed, wringing it out and wrapping it around himself so that he looked like a stained Nero.

"Yes, here they are," George said, wrinkling his nose. "They smell of cheese!"

"Of course they do! I've had them in my drawers – what do you expect!" Ivor said.

"Why didn't you tell me? George asked.

"I didn't want you rummaging around in my undies!" Ivor said indignantly.

"Yes, you're right – we don't need them," said George, dropping them on the floor and wiping his hand on his shirt. "You look just like Socrates!" he added.

"I always fancied myself as a philosopher actually," Ivor added. "You know, I had the brains and didn't use them. Still, it's part of my giving nature to help mankind, so medicine has always been a calling. I just thank God for making me such a tremendous person."

"Unbelievable," chimed Doctor Stumpf.

"Thank you, Ronald!" said Mallard

"Right then," George said, slapping his hands together and rubbing them in anticipation.

"Right then, what?" Ivor asked, looking at George blankly.

"I don't know! You're the philosopher!" George bleated.

"First, let's go and sit down on our sofa," Ivor suggested, wandering into the living room and sitting himself down. "God, my head hurts as well!" he mumbled.

"As well as what!" George asked.

"Uh, as well as ... um, Oh, God, as well as ... yours, of course!" Ivor finally said with relief.

"So, what do you think, Ivor?" George said, sitting on the sofa opposite.

"Well, I think all the furniture's gone missing," he reasoned.

"And my lovely Clivella!" Ronald added, screwing his face in grief.

"And the not-so-lovely Nurse Conwy," George said, causing Ivor to give an involuntary shudder.

"I think, and let me run this idea by you, that the furniture has been stolen," Ivor said cleverly.

"And, therefore, whoever stole the furniture must have stolen Nurse Conwy and Clivella as well," George posited.

"Brilliant!" Ivor replied, slapping his hands together then extending the right hand to shake with George to congratulate him on his incisive perception.

"You don't think that woman who was selling stuff at the fayre had anything to do with it, do you? I didn't like the look of her at all" George said.

"Could be, could be. One thing's for sure, we can't get the justice involved in any of this," Ivor said, squeezing the bridge of his nose between two fingers.

"Why not?" George asked.

"Because, dimwit, they're going to ask why we didn't witness it and why we didn't stop them. What are we going to say? 'I'm sorry, Sir, I was manacled to a bed, my friend was trying to shag a bearded lady in a dress whilst my two other compatriots were comparing the subtle qualities of some ridiculously named cocktails."

"We can't afford to jeopardise our good name," Ronald concurred.

"Oh, God, why did this happen to me! I never asked to be born," Ivor wailed, standing up and wringing his hands.

"Oh, cheer up, Ivor, it's not all bad. At least you had a night of passion! Think of poor Ronald. He's had all his things stolen and he didn't even get the memory of a night of love as a bit of a sweetener," said Lindsey.

"I don't call my encounter a 'night of passion', I assure you! It was more akin to being beaten up, only slightly less pleasurable ... hang on a minute!" Ivor blurted, suddenly interrupting himself. "We've still got that other little problem as well, haven't we!"

There were vacant faces all around, even though Ivor was pointing at the window.

"Eldritch, remember?" Ivor said in exasperation.

"Oh, no!" George said, running to the window with Ivor.

"He's gone!" Ivor exclaimed, looking at the dent in the cobbles where once had lain Eldritch's mortal remains.

"Maybe old Jones from the glue factory has taken him to melt him down," Ronald suggested, still staring at the floor in regret.

"We can but hope, Doctor Stumpf, although with my luck he's probably up on the roof as we speak, stripping the lead," Ivor said.

"What was that?" George asked, leaning back out of the window.

"What was it?" asked Ivor.

"I don't know," George answered, thrusting his head out of the open window just in time for a large strip of lead to catch him in the back of the neck and pull him into the street.

"You get back in here this instant, young man!" Ivor demanded. "Running around the streets in your drawers! It was bad enough having you on the roof in the buff, without you spoiling our good name by doing it in the street!"

George clambered to his feet and ran to the front door. In a few seconds, he was back in the house.

"God, that was a close thing! Mrs Jones almost saw me!" George said, pretending to fling sweat from his brow.

"Anyway, back to more pressing things. Who's stolen the furniture, and where have Nelly ... uh, I mean Nurse Conwy ... and Clivella gone?" Ivor said thoughtfully.

"So, what have we got? We have an empty house and two missing people. From this, we can deduce that either a lot of people stole our furniture *and* the two women, or that the two women worked very hard and stole it all themselves," Ivor reasoned.

"Or both," Lindsey added.

"Or both, as you say, Lindsey," Ivor accepted.

"It's demons! They drove us to drink and fornicate. Now they've taken everything we own!" Ronald howled, falling to his knees and pretending to pray.

"Then again," Ivor reasoned, "we have Ronald's idea."

"I didn't like to mention it before, Ivor, but even though I was drunk last night, and in an unconscious state, I vaguely remember hearing some very funny noises. Lots of grunts and snorts, a bit of screaming and howling as well," George added, looking at Ronald who now had his eyes screwed tightly shut, silently mouthing prayers for his sinful soul, his hands clasped together in front of him.

"Yes, well ... uh ... I really don't think *that's* too important," Ivor said, turning red.

"Hang on, what's that? Look, Ivor, it's another letter," George said, spying a soiled piece of paper that peeped out from under Ronald's cushion and was only visible now that Ronald had fallen to his knees in prayer.

"Well, come on then! Read it!" Ivor said impatiently.

"Dear All, I have been robbing you for months but you were too stupid to realise. Do you really think I enjoyed being your Nurse or pretending I liked that halfwit George? I just wanted to get one of you in a compromising position so that I could blackmail you. Then I met Clive at the fayre the other night when selling all your medical equipment and we decided that we'd clean you out at our first opportunity. I knew last night would be the night, as Clive had seen you all drinking at the fayre and I know Ivor can't handle his drink and that the evening would end with you losers passing out. Eldritch was in on it too. PS, Clive says to tell Ronald that he's a crap kisser," George read, folding the letter in two as he finished.

"Can you believe it!" Ivor said. "Me not handle my drink? I've never heard such rubbish."

"I'm the best kisser! *Nobody* kisses better than me!" Ronald added.

"Hmm, it's all a bit of a mystery, if you ask me," George pondered. "What I'm wondering is who wrote this letter. If we knew that, we'd have our man. My money is still on that woman we saw at the fayre. I didn't like the look of her."

"George, it was Nurse Conwy," Ivor answered.

"I'm not so sure. I think you're jumping to conclusions," George said, thinking himself jolly wily for being more thorough in his conclusions than his brother. "Why do you say that?"

"Because the writer of the letter says she hated being our Nurse and having to pretend she fancied you!" Ivor said in astonishment. "Surely that should narrow it down! If it said that she hated pretending to fancy you, we could narrow it down to one person given no one else does, but given she's our Nurse and the person that pretended to fancy you then I think it's pretty obvious who it is. That said, there's still something I don't get - we didn't see anyone

144

selling medical equipment other than the woman that looked like Nurse Conwy.

"And Clive says Doctor Stumpf is a crap kisser!" George shouted mockingly, looking at Ronald as he pulled a variety of faces, all of them variants on the theme of sucking lemons.

"Let me see that letter," Ivor said, snatching the paper from George's hands. "What's this 'PTO' at the bottom?"

"I didn't see that," said George, slumping to the floor as Ronald's dentures caught him squarely on the temple. "Oh, no! Oh, no, please!" Ivor said, collapsing onto the sofa, the open letter falling from his hand to the floor.

"What is it?" George asked, picking himself up and rubbing his head. "Our father and your mother are coming to visit us. They want to make sure that the money they're investing in you is being wisely spent. Well, that's really shagged it!"

"Mummy and daddy coming here? Oh, wonderful! How exciting! I can't wait to show them all the things I've bought and all the medical equipment I've amassed," George said excitedly.

"Well, unless you know where it all is, halfwit, you're not going to be able to, are you!" Ivor said angrily

"Tis but a trifle, Ivor. Doctor Stumpf has the house and all its contents insured. I know this, as

I've sent him the money myself every month," George replied nonchalantly.

"Oh, you do, do you? Care to explain, Doctor Stumpf?" Ivor said, arching an eyebrow.

"I spent it all on filthy woodcuts from Scandinavia. Eldritch has contacts over there," Ronald answered flatly.

"Oh, God!" Ivor said, burying his face in his hands.

"When are they coming?" George asked, excitedly. Ivor picked up the letter and scrutinised it for a date.

"Oh, God, they're coming tomorrow!" he wailed. "George, I can't even remember the name of that mother of yours. I've always known her as 'that dreadful woman who deprived me of what was rightfully mine'."

"It's Francesca - Lady Francesca - although everyone in the family tends to call her Franny for short," George answered.

"Fanny?" Doctor Stumpf asked, the word having roused him for his reverie.

"No, *Franny*! We must try and remember that as I don't want any more embarrassing cock-ups. Still, none of this helps us out of our current dilemma. Namely, we have virtually no clothes, hardly any furniture and no medical supplies," Ivor said woefully.

146

"What excuse can we give? Two were drunk, Doctor Stumpf was busy kissing a man in a dress and you too tied up to stop everything we own being stolen from under our flippin' noses!" George pondered.

"I didn't know it was a bloke!" Ronald ranted.

"Neither did I, but how many women have you seen that hairy - and with an Adam's apple!" Ivor commented.

"My sister! My mother! Anyway, I liked her for the person she was," Ronald explained.

"He's *so* dreamy!" Lindsey said, looking at Stumpf, his eyes twinkling in admiration.

"That's not strictly true, is it! You only liked *her* because she was the first person to give you a snog since old Jones' Jack Russell was bitten by that adder and you said you thought the snake had bitten its tongue so you had to suck out the poison!" Ivor remonstrated.

"No, that's where you're wrong! It was a wasp and not a snake. Now who's looking stupid!" Ronald said smugly.

"Look, this is getting us nowhere. Ronald, can you get the house insurance paperwork? As soon as we get that cashed, we can get some new furniture and things," said George.

"Doctor Stumpf to you!" Ivor sighed. "Try and understand, George, Ronald was lying when he took your money. There is no insurance and he spent all your money on himself."

George looked at Ivor for a moment, then at Ronald, who narrowed his eyes and looked back in the hope that such an expression made him look focussed and determined.

"Oh, right. What are we going to do then?" George said cheerily.

"George, you're not really like other men, are you?" Ivor commented.

"That's what they used to say to me at boarding school. 'George', they used to say, 'you're not like all the other boys'. I knew then I was special and that little something extra I had could really open things up for me," George effused.

"That's what Ronald's girlfriend must have thought," Ivor said, bursting out laughing and elbowing Ronald in the ribs. "Look, as stupid as George is, we do need a contingency plan. We've got until tomorrow morning to think of something, otherwise it's going to look pretty bad when Sir Richard and Fanny ...,"

"Franny," George said, interrupting his brother.

"Alright, Franny, arrives. Now, any suggestions?" Ivor asked, looking around the room optimistically.

"I have a suggestion!" said George.

"Excellent, this is more like it, now we're really getting somewhere! Yes, George, what's your suggestion?" Ivor asked.

"Only joking," George said sheepishly.

"I have an idea," Ronald said. "Why don't we invite a lot of other men to come here and we can all sit around talking about what it really feels like to be a man in our underwear. It will be a bonding experience."

"I couldn't agree more!" exclaimed Lindsey.

"I can't see it catching on," Ivor said diplomatically. "After all, I know two of you and don't really like seeing you in your undies, so God knows how horrific the experience would be for a stranger."

"We could get a lodger in!" suggested George.

"Brilliant," Ivor said. "George, you've done it again. It's not hard to see we're from the same stock. Naturally intelligent, you know."

"Hang on, you've had all your clothes stolen, all your medical equipment was stolen and all the furniture stolen. You have one day to replace it all. How much were you thinking of charging this lodger for one night's accommodation in a bare room?" Lindsey asked.

"Damn! I knew there'd be a drawback somewhere," said Ivor in annoyance.

"Let's hire out Doctor Stumpf as a hitman!" George suggested.

"No good. How long are those teeth going to last him, the way he's been chucking them around? No, the way I see it now is that we've got no other choice other than to be honest about this," said Ivor. Ronald shuddered at the word 'honest'.

"But what if they stop my allowance? I'll have to actually start working for a living!" said George, curling himself up in disgust.

"And if they do that I'll never get my hands on your cash ... er ... I mean ... oh crap ... you'll never get your hands on your cash," Ivor said, blushing a deep red.

"But I can't see a way out," George mumbled. "If only we hadn't had those gins at the fayre."

"It was you giving us all a *Knee Trembler* that did it," said Ivor.

"Oh right, blame me, why don't you! It was you that sacrificed yourself on the altar of decadence!"

"How dare you! I've got a good mind to take my belt off to you!" Ivor said affronted.

"You can't do that," Lindsey advised.

"Don't you tell me what I can and can't do. I won't be spoken to like that in my own home," Ivor said, standing up as if to make his gesture all the more defiant.

"You can't because you don't have a belt, nor britches, boots or a waistcoat. In fact, you've no clothes at all, remember?" said Lindsey.

"Then I'll ... take off *his* belt to you," Ivor said, moving to the window and pointing at a man walking past in the street below.

"Go on then!" George encouraged.

"I will! Just see if I don't," Ivor said, beginning to lose his nerve.

"You haven't got the guts!" Ronald added, beginning to make clucking noises.

"Right, that is it!" Ivor shouted. "Excuse me! Up here. Yes, hello. Might I borrow your belt, please? I wish to chastise my brother for saying it was my fault all our clothes were stolen because I'm a pervert," Ivor explained. "Well, that's charming! And the same to you, you old git!" he added, quickly drawing his head back into the room and wrapping the sheet tightly around him

"Well, what did he say?" chortled Lindsey.

"He said, uh ... that he was a little busy at the moment but would try and call around later, seeing as how it was me."

"Anyway, this still leaves us the problem of what we're going to do," whined George.

"I know what I'm going to do," Ivor said in annoyed resignation. "I'm going to just say balls to it!"

"Oh right," George said, a little taken aback.

"Well, what can we do? There's no way we can raise the cash and it's not as if we can make one or two rooms look full by taking furniture from some of the others, is there?" Ivor said in resignation.

"Couldn't we use Lindsey's house, saying that it's our new surgery?" George said, directing the remark more as a question to Lindsey than a reply to Ivor.

"No can do. I live in a garret, and you're not going to convince anyone that three Doctors are practising from one room," Lindsey replied.

"Does anyone have any idea of the time? Since I don't have a watch either, I don't even know what day it is," Ivor confessed.

"No, my watch has gone as well," Lindsey said.

"And mine," said George.

"Mine too," Ronald added.

"I tell you what would be really funny though, Ivor!" George said, suddenly laughing.

"I'm glad you can find something amusing, George but pray, do tell me what would be *really* funny?"

"If you really didn't know what day it was and that Sir Richard and Lady Francesca were coming today," he giggled.

"Oh yes. That's about as funny as a Shakespeare comedy. Don't even joke about such things ..." Ivor began, before being interrupted by a loud and officious bang at the door.

"Oh, no! That would be just too cruel a coincidence," he continued, moving to a side window that afforded a view of the steps that led to the front door.

"Well?" George asked.

"Balls! It's them. What's her name?" Ivor said, his eyes beginning to bulge and a large vein in his temple to throb.

"Who?" asked George vacantly.

"Your flippin' mother!" Ivor said, grabbing George by the throat and shaking him back and forth.

"Oh, is it mummy? It's Francesca. Franny, you know, Fanny with an 'r'." George replied, as his tongue began lolling from his mouth and his face turning as strange a colour as Doctor Stumpf's.

"Fanny with an 'r'. Fanny with an 'r', Fanny with an 'r'," Ivor muttered to himself, desperately trying to remember the name so that the first meeting in years with George's mother might be a success and that he might be able to ingratiate himself into the family and, most importantly, move him a step closer to the Uppham millions. "George, answer the door," Ivor barked, all the while still muttering the name: "Fanny with an 'r', Fanny with an 'r'."

"Mummy! Daddy!" George said pulling open the heavy door and greeting his parents with affectionate hugs, despite wearing nothing but his underwear.

"George," nodded Sir Richard.

"Hello darling, aren't you a little cold?" asked Lady Francesca, kissing George on the cheek.

"Father," Ivor oiled in sycophantic salutation, extending towards his father a hand which was dutifully received and a firm shake exchanged. Ivor smiled at Lady Francesca and took her hand, bowing as he did so, not noticing that Doctor Stumpf had arisen from his torpor and taken Sir Richard by the arm.

"Your Fanny is *so* beautiful," Ronald whispered to Sir Richard.

I Love Your Money!

"I beg your pardon!" said Sir Richard.

"Fanny - I know words. I have the best words," Ronald said. "What are the oranges of that really beautiful name?"

"Oranges?" said Sir Richard, moving closer to his wife.

"He means origins," Ivor explained, looking nervously around the foyer as every other face looked back at him blankly. "My colleague must be thinking of Princess Fanny of Nambia. Do you know her? I shouldn't really boast that she's a patient of Doctor Stumpf's, but she is. I suppose your rare beauty must have reminded him of her for just a moment," Ivor said, his eyes narrowing.

"Phew, well done, Ivor," said George.

"And this is Doctor Ronald Stumpf, the senior Doctor in the practice," Ivor said, making a few introductions. "And this is Lindsey Grayson, a toilet trader who seems to have become fond of the place!" he laughed.

"Well, George, I now see this is how you've been spending your allowance!" Sir Richard said, looking around the room at the bare boards, three grown men in their underwear and one in a stained sheet.

"Well, we've had a bit of trouble with the locals," George began.

"Yes, we were all called out to a fight that broke out at the Undertakers and Gravediggers Annual Gala. Apparently, someone stole the spade that was to have been the first prize in the raffle. God, it was like the French Revolution in there," Ivor explained.

"Yes, there were all these aristocrats' heads on spikes and they were guillotining people," George added enthusiastically, exploring the theme.

"Alright, don't overdo it," Ivor hissed, as discreetly as possible. "But that was in the real revolution, of course," he laughed, one more directing his comments to the assembled group.

"And there was need of a toilet salesman at this dreadful event?" asked Lady Francesca.

"Well ... uh, I almost shat myself," George said, helpfully.

"And? I take it this story goes some way to explaining your current circumstances?" Sir Richard said, looking Ivor up and down and ignoring George's comment as best he could.

"Of course! Of course! I'm just thinking," laughed Ivor, screwing up his face and looking at the ceiling in the hope of divine intervention.

"We were there so long that when we got home, all our furniture had been stolen by some callous rapscallions who knew we were out caring for the injured," George suggested.

"Brilliant, George! Yes, that was it! In serving humanity in our humble status as carers for the needy, we were burgled," Ivor said, shaking hands with George and giving him a pat on the back.

"You lot might have been, but I certainly wasn't. I've not been burgled in years," Lindsey said indignantly.

"That's burgled, Lindsey! B-u-r-g-1-e-d," Ivor spelt out the word. "As when one has all their possessions stolen from them."

"Ah right, I thought you meant ... no matter," Lindsey added, embarrassed at the misunderstanding.

"I see, I see," said Sir Richard, pondering the story.

"Then what happened to your clothes?" asked Lady Francesca.

"Oh crap!" Ivor said through gritted teeth. "Yes, George, what did happen to our clothes?"

"Um ... uh ... we were beaten and robbed and left by the roadside to die and if it hadn't been for the Samaritan on his way from Damascus to Jerusalem, we'd have all died," George blurted out, evidently caught on the hop.

"Ha! Ha! Ha! No, no, because that's a Biblical story, George!" Ivor said, resting his hand on George's shoulder and pinching his neck.

"Oh yes, sorry!" George said, drawing down the corners of his mouth and blushing.

"No, I've got it! The fight was so nasty and brutal that all our clothes were either torn from us or covered in blood," Ivor said.

"So, what you're saying is, you now have no clothes or furniture?" said Sir Richard.

"That's about the size of it," Ivor answered.

"As the actress said to the bishop!" George began before being stopped by Ivor with a well-aimed elbow to the side of the head.

"And your medical equipment?" Sir Richard asked, taking a handkerchief from the pocket of his britches and mopping his brow.

"All gone, I'm afraid," Ivor confirmed.

"So, none of you were drunk then?" Lady Francesca asked, half laughing and half-serious.

"Mumsie, I'm shocked!" George said. "Do you really think that all along I've been telling you a lie? It's exactly as it happened. We were called out to the … uh … Navvies and Drunkards monthly bash and a fight broke out when someone stole a pickaxe," George said indignantly. "That was the story you gave them, wasn't it?" he whispered to Ivor as an aside.

"This really isn't good news at all," said Sir Richard. "Firstly, let's get you some clothes. I never liked the sight of naked men at the best of times, especially when they look like him," he added, gesturing to Doctor Stumpf who, wearing nothing but his drawers, now resembled a week-old party balloon with a head.

"Obviously none of you is really in a position to come with us, so I suppose we shall have to go on our own and come back with a selection for you," Lady Francesca suggested.

"Well, that went pretty smoothly," Ivor said as Lady Francesca and Sir Richard left and he closed the door behind them.

"Sweet as some nuts. We're home and dry!" added George.

"She's a lovely looking woman, your mother," Ronald said to George as he made squeezing gestures with his fingers.

"There you are, George, you could have Ronald as a stepfather!" Ivor laughed, watching George's nose wrinkle up as if an offensive smell had just passed underneath it.

"I'd rather not," George said.

"One thing does bother me, though," Ivor said, his forehead creasing as he tapped his chin with his index finger.

"Eh?" George grunted as he made himself comfortable on the sofa.

"Why have they come here? Come on, how often do we see them! Sir Richard couldn't wait to pay off my mother when your mother fell pregnant and as soon as I was old enough, he kicked me out. If it hadn't been for the good fortune of meeting the amazing Doctor Stumpf and his snake oil business then who knows what might have become of me!" Ivor pondered.

"Hang on a moment! My life hasn't been all plain sailing you know! If I hadn't used my wit to con those that believe I'm a Doctor then who knows what could have become of me!" George argued.

"Yes, you could be sitting around in a house with no furniture, clothes or money. Imagine!" scoffed Lindsey.

"So, why are they here now?" Ivor pondered.

George put his elbow on his knee, clenched his fist and rested it against his forehead.

"Don't try and ponder as well, George, it doesn't become you. Remember those wise words you said to me at the fayre? 'Upstairs for thinking, downstairs for dancing¦'," Ivor said, spying George's attempts at mimicry that simply resembled a small child copying their parent without any knowledge or understanding of why.

"Yes, it is odd," George said wistfully.

"What?" Ivor asked, slightly annoyed that his train of thought had been interrupted.

"Why you never see a swallow in a tree. I reckon it's because they've got no feet. And what about mice, eh? I saw one crawl under a door once and the gap was no wider than the width of my pinkie fingernail! Now you try and tell me that a mouse has bones! Never!" George said. Ronald and Lindsey looked at George and then at one another in complete confusion.

"Yes, George. It's good to see that you're looking at this mystery from all possible angles. Might I be so bold, however, as to suggest that you're thinking a little *too* laterally?" Ivor said, smiling smugly, looking at Ronald and Lindsey as he spoke, whilst gesturing to George with his head. The pair of stony faces that greeted him, however, quickly turned Ivor's expression to one of thoughtful contemplation.

"Perhaps they're finally going to accept you as part of the family," Ronald suggested.

"Yes, maybe," Ivor said indifferently. "Perhaps they're going to give me some cash!" he added, and a greedy smile crossed his face as the thought suddenly came to him.

"Well, it looks like you might find out sooner than you think," Lindsey said, rising from his seat. "Here they come!"

"Lindsey, it's rude to stare!" Ivor said.

"Oh crap, they've seen me!" Lindsey said, trying to quickly duck from view, only to smash his head on the windowsill.

"Oh dear, that sounded painful!" said George, pursing his lips and taking a sharp intake of breath as the hollow ringing sound from Lindsey's head echoed about the room and his unconscious form slumped to a heap on the bare boards.

"Oh, that's just marvellous, isn't it!" Ivor said jutting out his bottom jaw and drawing his hands into upturned claws.

"Well, at least he might be his old self again when he wakes up. That bang on the head at the fayre turned him into a right one," George said.

As anticipated, there was a loud knock on the door and, once again, George opened it wide, clad only in his drawers.

"George, please! You'll be getting the company a bad name opening the door in such a way!" Lady Francesca protested.

"Well, here you are," Sir Richard said, draping a pile of new clothes over the back of the sofa. "Having you all dressed will be a start, at least."

"Bags I the green frock coat," George said, as Ivor made a snatch for it.

"Ha! Ha! I had my eye on that! Finders keepers, losers' weepers!" Ivor said, trying his best to squeeze himself into a coat that was obviously too small for him

"Dad, tell Ivor! He stole my coat," wailed George.

"There! A perfect fit," Ivor said, straining to pull the coat around him, even though the arms remained three or four inches above his wrists.

"No, it's mine!" George said, his mood suddenly turning from tears to anger as he jumped behind Ivor and tried to tear the coat from his back.

"No! You have the grey one. Grey suits you better - you're a grey sort of person!" Ivor hissed, writhing around under George's grip.

"No, you swine! You knew I wanted that coat! That's the only reason you wanted it."

"Rubbish! It's to bring out the beautifully understated green flecks in my eyes. I shall bestride the next Surgeon and Barber convention like a colossus with the flecks of my balls twinkling."

"Ooh, you don't need a coat to do that, Ducky," said Lindsey, rubbing his head and drawing himself up onto his haunches.

"It's Mallard! How many times have I got to tell you?" Ivor shouted, finally freeing himself from George's grip.

"Lindsey, you're back!" said George, pleased to see his new friend's old personality re-emerge.

"Why, have I been somewhere?" Lindsey asked, rubbing his temple and looking a little bemused. Only then did he realise he was almost naked, save for his drawers. "Oh, good heavens, where are my clothes? I say, we have been naughty boys, haven't we!"

"No. We were robbed and beaten, remember?" Ivor said emphatically.

"Were we? Oh, how dreadfully disappointing!" Lindsey replied, looking crestfallen.

"What's all this then? Why doesn't he remember?" Sir Richard said, beginning to smell a rat.

"Oh, you know. It's what we in medical circles call a 'softening of the brain'. I'm afraid he caught one fist too many last night and can't remember a thing," Ivor explained.

"Ooh, sounds like I missed a real ding-dong!" Lindsey said, with a twinkle in his eye.

"Well, come on, children! Get dressed. Sir Richard and I have some news for you," Lady Francesca said, ushering the group toward the neatly piled heap of attire.

"I can't take off my underwear in front of a lady," Ronald said.

"You feel like that as well do you, Ronald?" Lindsey asked, resting a hand on Ronald's shoulder.

"Then I'd better wait for you in that room, over there," Lady Francesca said, moving towards Nurse Conwy's room before Ivor had a chance to intercede. As Lady Francesca opened the door, a loud braying echoed around the empty room as the donkey, previously the soul of discretion, saw its chance of freedom and bolted into the living room.

"Excuse my noisy ass," said Ivor.

"I've heard worse!" Lindsey added.

"What the devil!" Sir Richard shouted in disbelief as the donkey came to halt and relaxed, now that it found itself in such an urbane soiree.

"Those burglars! They must think of this as some sort of sick joke!" protested Ivor furtively, scanning the room from the corner of his eyes.

"Perhaps it's a calling card! You know, some burglars, when they burgle a place leave a card behind. Maybe ours left a donkey," George suggested helpfully.

"Oh yes, I can just see that, can't you? A swag bag under one arm and a donkey under the other," Ivor said sarcastically.

"Maybe they stopped to rehearse A Midsummer Night's Dream and left their Bottom behind," Ronald suggested.

"Oh, no! Believe me, I know a good Bottom when I see one," said Lindsey, "and that isn't a good one even by the most degraded of standards!"

"Look, none of you is making this very easy for me," Ivor said, leaning over to his friends and hissing the words harshly through clenched teeth.

"It's alright. No need to clench your teeth with us," Ronald said.

"Definitely! Just relax, I always say," Lindsey added.

"This bed is soaking!" Lady Francesca shouted from behind the closed door.

"Those depraved animals!" Ivor shouted in disgust, emphasising the abomination with his arms.

"That was Ivor," George said.

"What!" exclaimed Sir Richard, becoming ever more suspicious.

"No, George, it wasn't, now was it!" said Ivor, kicking George in the small of the back, given George was now sitting on the floor pulling on his stockings.

"Yes, it was, don't you remember, Ivor?"

"Uh, no!" said Ivor, going red and shifting uneasily.

"Yes, you do. Last night ..." George continued, as Ivor winced. "All those tears you shed when you realised that all our worldly goods had been stolen and that we had nothing to show for our endeavours other than a place in heaven, and how the few pennies we'd saved for the orphans would now have to go on a few sticks of furniture instead."

"Brilliant! Yes, I remember it all now. That's exactly how it was! Funny the things you forget when you're tired from helping the needy," Ivor said, leaning over George and giving him a congratulatory pat on the shoulder.

"My boys! I am standing proud," Sir Richard began, bringing his index finger to his lips as he saw Lindsey about to speak. "As soon as you are dressed, I want to sit down with you both and get something off my chest, something I meant to tell you when first you began working together," he added, pacing up and down. Ivor and George looked at one another with some concern and quickly finished dressing. "I should like, if you don't mind, to speak to my sons in private," Sir Richard said to Ronald and Lindsey. "Could give us just a little privacy for a moment or two?"

"Of course. I know how important a little privacy can be when men get together," Lindsey added.

"Thank you, chaps. I'm sure George and Ivor will tell you in due course, but for their sake, I think they should be able to choose the time," Sir Richard said with sincerity, as Ronald and Lindsey left the room, leaving the fully attired George and Ivor standing awkwardly in front of him, neither knowing what fate awaited them.

"I'll just go and get Lady Francesca," said Sir Richard, returning a moment later with his wife.

"Shall I begin?" Sir Richard asked his wife, who nodded her acquiescence. "I know this involves you both, but it will probably come as a bigger shock to Ivor. Ivor, you've always known I was your real father. What you haven't known is that Lady Francesca is also your real mother." The colour drained from Ivor's face as he looked from Sir Richard to Lady Francesca, then blankly back at Sir Richard.

"I don't understand," he murmured. "Was I given away or something?"

"Yes," Sir Richard said honestly.

"Why?"

"Well, we just didn't like the look of you very much. We thought about keeping you and fattening you up for Christmas, but the turkey worked out cheaper," Sir Richard confessed.

"Well, thanks for dressing it up for me!" Ivor said indignantly. "You might have softened the blow by saying you were too young or you were too poor or that I'd been unplanned. Now I find out I lost by a short neck to Reggie the Rooster!"

"If it's any consolation, he was very tasty," Sir Richard added.

"And we did drink a toast to you," said Lady Francesca.

"Well, on the first Christmas anyway," Sir Richard clarified.

"This is bloody marvellous, isn't it?" stormed Ivor. "Hang on a minute ... if I'm legally your child that means, as the oldest, I'm entitled to the estates and that George is no longer the heir to the Uppham millions!"

"Yes, I suppose it does. We'd not thought of that," Sir Richard said, looking at his wife.

"I'm rich! Wa-hey! I'm rich! I always knew destiny had me marked out as special. Cock-a-bloody-doodle-do!" Ivor bellowed, running around the room making flapping motions with his arms.

"I must say, Ivor, you're taking this a lot better than I'd anticipated," Lady Francesca remarked.

"Lindsey, Ronald, come in, quickly!" Ivor laughed, running to the door and calling up the passage.

"What is it?" Ronald asked as he entered the room, followed by Lindsey a moment or two later.

"I'm rich! I'm on the gravy train at last! Can you believe it?" Ivor said, running on the spot and flapping his arms wildly.

"How come?" Lindsey asked.

"I'm the eldest son. George isn't the heir to the Uppham millions at all - I am! For the first time in my life, I really feel as if I'm getting somewhere," Ivor said excitedly.

"Hang on a minute," Ronald said. "You're not rich yet, are you?"

"What do you mean?" said Ivor, suddenly stopping his frantic movements and taking on a serious disposition.

"Well, you might be rich on paper, but you don't have a penny at the moment. Neither of them has left you anything - yet - on account of their still being alive," Ronald pointed out.

"Oh, bollocks!" Ivor shouted, staring at the floor. "Why does every silver lining have to have a cloud?" he muttered, moodily slouching into a chair.

"Well, I'm sorry if our still being alive is a disappointment to you," Sir Richard said, haughtily.

"S'alright, I suppose," said Ivor, sulking.

"Come on Ivor, it's not all bad. After all, what's the average age people live to these days? Forty? Fifty? Well, we can count our lucky stars that we haven't got very long to wait, have we?" George said, giving his brother's leg a shake. "I mean, look at him!" he said, pointing to his father. "He's seventy if he's a day, overweight, with a blood pressure problem and unless a complexion that shade of red is in fashion this season ... whilst her ..." George said tutting. "Well, what does she know about money? We can settle her down into a little gatehouse somewhere once the big cheese pops his clogs! Give her a few pounds a month and all the sherry she can drink and she won't grumble about a thing."

"Thanks, George. I know you're trying to be nice to me and that's very sweet of you, but it really is awful being so near to all that cash and yet so far," Ivor said, wiping a tear from his eyes.

"Well! How sharper than a serpent's tooth it is to have an ungrateful child," said Sir Richard.

"Ooh, listen to her!" said Lindsey.

"I'm sorry, Father," said Ivor. "And an apology to you as well ... Mother," he added humbly.

"After all, you haven't given us any cash to buy some new equipment yet," George added.

"Yes, thank you, George! I was coming to that!" Ivor said, kicking George on the ankle.

"Is that all you want from us?" Lady Francesca said in exasperation, looking to her husband to see if he shared her indignation.

"Well, I like that! You were the one that gave me up me in favour of a chicken," Ivor fumed.

"It was a turkey, actually," Sir Richard said pedantically.

"Oh Ivor, I'd have never passed you up for a turkey!" Lindsey said sympathetically. "A goose maybe ..."

"Alright, thank you, everybody! I think we've established that in God's great scheme of things I'm vying neck and neck with an assortment of poultry, but if anyone's trying to make me feel better here it isn't working," stormed Ivor.

"He's very good, isn't he!" Ronald whispered to Lindsey.

"Excuse me! Excuse me! Do you think this is some sort of an act? I come *this* close to inheriting a fortune and I can now see it drifting away from me by ... oh, I don't know … words fail me," Ivor said slumping into a chair. "George, put the kettle on and make some tea, can you?"

"I can't, Ivor," George replied.

"Oh, don't tell me! You've broken your leg trying to get up again?"

"No, it's not that this time."

"A hernia?" Ivor asked, his curiosity aroused.

"No, not that either."

"Elephantiasis of the scrotum?" Ivor asked, closing his eyes in defeat.

"No. Do you want me to tell you? We haven't got any tea. It was stolen, remember?" George said, pleased that he had been able to impart some information of which his brother had been ignorant.

"And the cups, kettle, milk, sugar and tea strainer," Ronald added.

"Not forgetting the stove," Lindsey pointed out.

"I've seen quite enough of this circus," Sir Richard said, taking his wife by the hand. "I'm not going to give either of you a penny! You're a pair of lunatics and as soon as I get home, I'm disinheriting the pair of you. If this is what education does for you, God help us!"

"We're the new elite, getting the country back on its feet," said George proudly.

"And where do you two think you're going?" Ivor said, jumping from his seat and hurdling a sofa, blocking the door as Lady Francesca and Sir Richard made advances to leave. "So long as there's a penny in that fat wallet of yours, you're not going anywhere," he added, waving his index finger menacingly.

"Well, it's nice to know all you want us for is our money! What about love?" asked Lady Francesca.

"I love your money!" Ivor said greedily. "Besides, if you never gave us any love, how can you expect us to start giving *you* love now? You bought your freedom from us! Well, now it's time to pay! Lindsey, grab his fat wad ... and no smutty remarks! Ronald, you make sure they have a carriage to get them away from here. George, you just stare vacantly into space - I shouldn't want you to break the habit of a lifetime!"

"This is scandalous! What about the bonds between parents and children?" stammered Sir Richard as he was relieved of his wallet.

"Scandalous? Do you really think so? Don't give me that! You only bought these clothes to ease your guilty conscience and the money you ploughed into this business wasn't so much philanthropy as you seeing an opportunity to make a quick buck out of poor stupid George. Well not me, I'm too smart for that and rumbled your little game, didn't I?" Ivor said, thumbing through the banknotes.

"Shall I tie them up?" asked Lindsey.

"Yes, you better had," Ivor said, now fancying himself as a swashbuckling highwayman.

"I shan't be a moment then," Lindsey said, leaving the room for a minute or so. "All done," he said on his return.

"Eh? I thought you said you were going to tie them up?" Ivor asked.

"I have," Lindsey said.

"I meant these two," Ivor said raising his eyes to the ceiling and pointing at his parents. "God, I shudder to think what you've been tying up."

"Oh! Them as well? Sorry, I'll just go and get some rope," Lindsey said, walking bow-legged from the room, leaving Ivor and Ronald sharing confused looks with one another and George staring from the window in his usual manner.

"Right, now tie *them* up," Ivor commanded as Lindsey returned with the rope.

"All done," Lindsey said, having quickly accomplished his task.

"Thought you could outfox us, did you? Thought you were smarter than us, did you? Get in there, you mercenary pair, and I don't want to hear a peep out of you whilst you think about the way you've treated poor George and me," Ivor said, pulling a door open and pushing Lady Francesca and Sir Richard through it.

"Ha-ha! Job done," Ivor said as he closed the door and dusted his hands.

"Ivor," said Lindsey

"Not now Lindsey. Let me savour the moment. It's not often I've had any power in my life. Now I have money and revenge, and it tastes pretty damn good," Ivor said, slapping his lips.

"It is quite important," Lindsey insisted.

"Oh Lindsey, what is it, for God's sake?" Ivor snapped.

"You do know that the door you just opened was the front door and that you bundled them both out into the street, don't you?" Lindsey said, wincing as he spoke.

"What! Oh, bollocks!" Ivor shouted as he opened the door, only to see Sir Richard and Lady Francesca hot-footing it down the road.

"Bollocks! Bollocks! Bollocks! It's your fault," he said, reaching out a hand and slapping George around the side of the head.

How Much for a Shag?

"What was that for?" asked George, rubbing his head.

"It's for driving our parents away," Ivor said.

"How did I do that then?"

"Oh, cheer up, Ivor. Things could be worse. At least you have some clothes on your back and a wallet full of money," Lindsey reasoned.

"You're right!" Ivor snapped, walking backwards and forwards whilst tapping his chin with his index finger. "For the moment I'm rich, but it does present us with a problem. Namely, no more allowances."

"What?" George wailed, rising to his feet. "No more allowances! That means I'll have to work for a living! Oh, God, what a thought! What else will I be expected to do? Have a few starving children? Drink pints of beer? No! I won't do it."

"But hang on a minute! You and Ronald have been Quacks for years. You must have a bob or two stashed away in a bank somewhere," Lindsey said.

"How dare you! You wander in here with your cheap-jack latrines and then have the nerve to call me a Quack!" Ivor said, his face glistening with contempt.

"Banks are for swine," Ronald added.

"And as Doctor Stumpf's well-observed argument points out, banks aren't the place for wages earned in caring for the sick. It is too holy a calling to be sullied amongst the rank and file of foul businessmen and those dreadful working classes," Ivor said, angrily.

"So, neither of you have any money at all?" Lindsey asked in amazement.

"Not a penny," Ivor said haughtily.

"The beauty of me is that I'm very rich ... people love me! And you know what? I've been very successful. Everybody loves me!" Ronald added, taking his teeth out and wiping them on the arm of his coat.

"Still, I can see one pertinent thing you've pointed out, Lindsey," Ivor said smiling.

"What's that?"

"I have money now. Therefore, let us eat and drink, for tomorrow we shall die!" Ivor shouted, jumping onto the sofa with one foot resting on its arm and his arm raised aloft in proud defiance.

"It's always great when someone else is paying! We can spend, spend, spend!" Ronald said, rubbing his greedy hands together.

"Hang on! What's all this 'we' business? This money is mine!" Ivor said, clutching the wallet close to his chest.

"And mine!" reasoned George.

How Much for a Shag?

"Well ... oh ... oh balls ... I suppose so. I'll split it with you seventy thirty," Ivor said, pouting and looking exasperated.

"That's not fair! It's eighty twenty or nothing," George argued.

"Alright then - nothing!" Ivor said, jumping from the sofa and holding the wallet as high as he could, out of George's reach.

"You know what I meant!" George said, jumping up and down and trying to snatch the wallet from Ivor's hand.

"Well George, you drive a hard bargain, but eighty twenty it is then," Ivor conceded.

"Ha-ha! See? I can be ruthless when I want to be," George scoffed.

"Oh, I see that all too clearly now, George," Ivor answered, sitting on the floor and opening the wallet. "My God, there's over fifty pounds in here!"

"So that's ..." George said, screwing up his face and looking aloft in concentration.

"That's ten pounds for you and forty for me, which leaves us with thirty-pound left over," Ivor said.

"And that's mine," Ronald said quickly.

"Is it? Well, you'd better have it then," Ivor answered, looking at Ronald, recognising something wasn't quite right but not knowing what.

"Right then, Ivor, what are you going to spend the money on?" George asked.

"Well, I suppose we'd better think about furnishing this place," Ivor said, looking around him at the bare walls and floors. "We certainly need some tables, chairs, desks and things. Anyone got any suggestions?"

"I vaguely remember reading about a furniture sale going on in the indoor market in town today. I didn't pay much attention but I'm sure it was today," Lindsey said.

"Then I think that should be our first port of call," Ivor said decisively. "We do, however, need to set ourselves a budget. What shall we say to furnish the entire place? Fifty pounds? Split that three ways and that leaves us having to pay ..." Ivor put the palm of his hand over his eyes and stuck out his tongue in concentration.

"Here's my money," Ronald said, throwing a few coins into Ivor's lap.

"Oh right, so if I put in my money, that just leaves George to put in his ..." Ivor grimaced.

"Seventy pounds," said Ronald.

"Yes!" Ivor said, suddenly illuminated.

"Is that right?" George asked, looking suspiciously at Ivor and Ronald.

"Of course, it is," barked Ronald.

"No, I'm not having that," George said dismissively. "Three seventy pounds does not make fifty pounds".

"You know, you're right, George! You should be giving us eighty, not seventy. Good job you noticed, George. You're too sharp for Ronald and me," Ivor said.

"You'd have to get up pretty early in the morning to catch me out," George said triumphantly.

"I can see that, George. We're obviously going to have to be very careful around you, aren't we Ronald?" Ivor said, winking and grinning inanely at Ronald who looked back stony-faced. Ivor immediately lost his look of glee and took on a stern, serious countenance.

"We might as well be off then!" Lindsey said, rising to his feet.

"Do you want to take the lead?" Ivor replied.

"Well, it's not my usual role, but what the hell! I can throw caution to the wind just this once," Lindsey replied.

"I hate this indoor market," George said, as the group walked down the street. "It always smells like strong cheese and rotting fish on a hot summer's day."

"Is that what it is, is it? I'd wondered what it was. I'd always thought it was Mrs Jones who run that little knocking shop up Pit Street," Ivor replied.

"It is her as well," Ronald added. "She's usually there stocking up on those little nibbles I like before I ..." his voice trailing off as he realised how large a hole he was digging himself.

"Please, can we change the subject? My constitution isn't all it should be today, and talk of food is making my stomach churn. My God, this is Wales, not the last days of Rome!" Lindsey said, holding his stomach as he spoke.

Very soon, the cold and imposing facade of the indoor market came into view. As they ascended its steps the sudden chill of the place made a startling contrast to the warmth of the sunny day outside.

"Ah, this is just the thing," said Ivor, looking around at all the various stalls laid out in front of him, each selling a variety of bric-à-brac that ranged from the smallest of ornaments to the largest of wardrobes and desks.

"Look, Ivor! There's that woman who was at the fayre. Remember? The one that looked like Nurse Conwy," said George excitedly.

"So it is. Let's go and see if she has any medical supplies. We could certainly do with a few now that all ours have gone," Ivor said, leading the group of three to the stall, Ronald having already absconded.

"Look at that! If I didn't know better, I'd say that was my wardrobe," said George, pointing to a large Dutch mahogany and marquetry affair, decorated in flowers, birds and ornate vases. "Look, it even has clothes in it that look just like mine," George said, opening the door and shaking his head in disbelief at such a coincidence.

"And to think the very same woman had stuff on her stall yesterday that was monogrammed with your initials," Ivor added, equally bemused.

"I don't like it at all, Ivor. It makes me think I've got a double somewhere and that he's going to come up and touch me and I'll explode or something," George said fearfully.

"That's science talking again!" said Ivor, looking around the stall.

"I don't believe it! I don't think there's anything on this stall that we didn't have one just like," he said, stroking his chin and shaking his head in astonishment.

"Are you sure you're not Nurse Conwy?" asked George.

"Get stuffed, halfwit," the woman said, taking a letter opener and pointing it threateningly at George's abdomen.

184

"You even talk like her! You really should have met our nurse," Ivor continued. "The similarity between you and her is uncanny."

"Yes, but she was stolen along with all our furniture when we got drunk last night," George confided.

"Yes, we all had a *Quickie* after a *Kiss Behind the Cowshed* from my brother," Ivor explained.

"Did we? God, I must have been drunk! I haven't been to a party like that since I was an undergraduate and Oscar Beckford and I joined the all-male acting club, just so we could attend their nymphs and satyrs' ball. Oh, to be the golden-haired Apollo I once was!" Lindsey said wistfully.

"Oh look, Ivor," George said, pointing at a pair of old paintings of a Cormorant. "Isn't that a Shag?" he tittered.

"Ah, yes," said Ivor, spying the object of George's fascination. "Excuse me, Miss ... Miss? How much for a Shag?" Ivor asked, leaning across the table.

"Same as it was last night ... uh," replied the woman, taking a sharp gasp as she realised she'd betrayed her cunning disguise.

"So, you *are* the real Nurse Conwy! What happened to the woman who had the stall at the fayre?" Ivor stammered, standing upright and pointing at Nurse Conwy as he spoke. "And perhaps you can tell us what the people who stole you have done with all our furniture? We're not Doctors for nothing, you know! We know how many beans make five and so does our friend, the toilet salesman," he added.

"Clive took it all, along with all your furniture," Nurse Conwy said contemptuously, looking Ivor up and down as she spoke.

"So, where is it all now then?" George asked, thinking himself a particularly hard interrogator.

Nurse Conwy looked at the array of goods on her table and then at the unenlightened faces of the three men in front of her.

"It was all stolen from us ... uh, him," Nurse Conwy said.

"Ha, I thought as ... much," George said, his sentence trailing to a whisper as it dawned on him that Nurse Conwy hadn't given the answer he'd anticipated.

"So, do you want to buy anything or not?" Nurse Conwy said, throwing her arms wide open and gesturing to all her wares.

"Not from you," Ivor said snobbishly. "I wouldn't be seen with rubbish like this in my house. I have standards to be maintained! Come, Lindsey, George! Let us away from this foul harridan."

"G'day gentleman," said one particularly scabrous individual maintaining a stall a few rows down from Nurse Conwy's. George couldn't help but stop and look at the array of exotic goods of Moorish and Middle Eastern origin.

"Hello!" said George cheerily. "This looks interesting," he said picking up a jug made from a human skull. "What's it made of?"

"Ah, I see that you are something of a dilettante," said the stallholder.

"Well, I'm not one to boast but I'm certainly glad that it shows," Ivor said, smiling broadly.

"What you have there, young Sir, is a jug that was once owned by John Dee, Magician and Alchemist to Elizabeth the First," said the stallholder, his walnut features looking as though they were about to crack at the exertion of speaking.

"Oh, go on!" said George.

"And here, Sir, we have a haunted wardrobe," the stallholder said, pulling a sheet off a particularly drab but large wardrobe.

"Ooh!" uttered George in childlike awe. "How much is it?"

"It's ten pounds, given it's a very special wardrobe."

"Ooh, I don't know. Will you take twelve?" George bartered.

"I don't know," the man answered, thanking his lucky stars. "Alright, you drive a hard bargain, but as I need the money, it's yours."

How Much for a Shag?

"Hooray!" said George, quickly parting with the last of his money, then giving the man his address and making delivery arrangements.

"Ivor! Lindsey! I've just bought a wardrobe!" George gushed, running up to his friends who had continued meandering from stall to stall when they had seen George waylaid in conversation.

"Which one?" Ivor asked excitedly.

"That little beauty there," George said, pointing.

"That's a bit ... crap, George. It's even got a crack in it! How much did you pay for it? I hope you haggled," Ivor said.

"Well, he wanted ten, but I haggled a bit and got it for twelve," George replied.

"You've not really grasped this haggling business, have you, George? You're supposed to haggle *down,* not up. It's to save you money. I still think twelve is very expensive, George. You should have offered him eleven," Ivor said paternally.

"Eleven? Are you crazy?" George said, a look of incredulity on his face. "You don't understand, Ivor. It's a haunted wardrobe," George explained, hoping the fact might justify the expenditure.

"So, you've spent all that money on an old wardrobe?" Ivor said, crossing his arms and looking down his nose as George visibly shrunk under the scrutiny.

"I'm a bit of a twat, aren't I!" George offered in defence.

"Yes. Still, if you want to spend the money I stole on rubbish, that's up to you. I'm still intrigued as to why you should want a haunted wardrobe in the first place," Ivor added.

"Oh, it'll be exciting! Imagine - a foul and unholy presence might come and haunt my britches ..."

"Nothing new there, then!" Ivor remarked.

"No, I think George might be onto something," Lindsey added. "Just last Wednesday I walked through that dark old graveyard in the centre of town and felt these rough hands all over me. Unfortunately, it was too dark to see who, or what, it was. I went back the following night but even though I waited around for hours I didn't get so much as a sniff!"

"Well, all I can say is *don't tell Ronald*. You know how he feels about ghosts and the supernatural," Ivor said. "And children come to think of it... and old people ... and people his age!"

"And men!" George added.

"And women, come to think of it," Ivor added nodding in agreement. "And exercise, windmills, foreigners, salads, dogs, sharks, vegetarians, cauliflower hidden in his mashed potatoes, single scoops of ice cream, umbrellas, chocolate cake that isn't beautiful, anyone from the borders - anyone who doesn't live in the same town as us, come to think of it! In fact, he probably doesn't like people that make wardrobes either, so it's not going to make much difference whether you tell him it's haunted or not!"

"Does he like anyone?" Lindsey asked in astonishment.

"His daughter. Money, obviously. Wait! There was one person a long time ago who lived a couple of streets away who he was simply indifferent to. I suppose that counts," Ivor recollected.

"And why did he like him?" Lindsey asked.

"He used to make cat o' nine tails for seamen, only his had bits of metal embedded in the lashes so that they were more painful," answered Ivor. "I think he thought they made better sailors once they'd had a good horsewhipping."

"And that's why sailors have rough backs!" added George.

"Oh fancy! I'd often wondered," Lindsey retorted.

"Talk of the devil!" George said. "Here's Doctor Stumpf. Hello Doctor Stumpf, have you bought anything?"

"Only this old whip," Ronald answered grimly, giving it a flick at some passing migrants.

"Did you haggle with him?" Ivor asked.

"Well, I did beat him down, in a manner of speaking," Ronald answered, a sinister smile flickering across his face for an instant before his usual expression returned and the moment passed. "Did you buy anything?"

"A few bits and pieces whilst George busied himself buying a wardrobe. I've bought a job lot of furniture, just to get the house full, rather than look around. We could spend weeks doing this and we now have the more pressing matter of actually working for a living and not simply living off the Uppham allowance that George was getting," Ivor said, noting the pain in the faces of George and Ronald as he mentioned the word 'work'.

"I've been meaning to ask you, Lindsey, how come you don't have to work?" said George.

"I do work, dear boy. Thing is, I'm a very good salesman who really likes to get close to his customers and the product he sells. In fact, the closer the better. I'll tell you this in confidence, there's big money in toilets for the right man," he whispered.

"Is there? I've never noticed. They certainly didn't teach us that in medical school!" George said in astonishment. Did either of you know that?" he asked Ronald and Ivor, both of who looked equally astounded.

How Much for a Shag?

"Are you sure about that, Lindsey? Money from waste?" Ivor asked.

"Ivor, perhaps you could get some more of those sausages that gave us all food poisoning! We'd be laughing all the way to the bank!" George said.

"Banks are for swine," Ronald said, evidently standing firm on the opinion he'd voiced earlier that day.

"Yes, a slight misunderstanding. Still, no matter. Shall we carry on or have we all seen enough?" Lindsey said, indicating he wished to continue browsing even if the others had seen enough.

"Well, I suppose we could have a little look around before we leave, now that we're here," Ivor said.

"I was hoping you'd say that! I'm looking for some soft furnishings for my boudoir," Lindsey said.

"Well, there's a stall," George said pointing and skipping off towards it.

"Anything particular in mind, Lindsey?" asked Ivor.

"Not really. So long as it's beautiful and a feast for the eye."

"Look at this pouffe, Lindsey," George said.

"Oh, you dear boy! You don't know how long I've been looking for one of these! Here, let me try it out," he said, taking the pouffe from George's grasp and placing it on the floor, whereupon he squatted down until fully recumbent on it. "I have very refined tastes when it comes to matters such as these," he said. "Too hard is wonderful to begin with but one quickly becomes sore - too soft and one simply slips out of the saddle, so to speak. One has to have a pouffe that is neither too hard nor too soft for one to be able to lie back and relax completely."

"How is it?" George asked.

"Far too hard, I'm afraid," Lindsey said, handing back the pouffe with a look of melancholy. "I used to believe that the harder the pouffe, the better. Age, however, has softened the recklessness of youth. Now I prefer comfort to the fleeting thrills of yore."

"Well, if we've all quite finished, we might as well go back to the house and await our deliveries," Ivor said, leading the little troupe from the building and back out into the warm sunshine of the day.

As the group made its way back to the house, Lindsey, George and Ivor walked a little way in front of Ronald, as he wanted to threaten children with his new whip and tell them that now they were seven years old it was time to set aside childish pleasures and get a job down the coal mine in which he had shares and *dig beautiful, clean coal*.

"Remember what I said about that wardrobe, George. Don't go mentioning the fact that it's haunted in front of Ronald. You know how these things upset him. He might only be looking for an excuse to become upset, but there's no sense in giving him something to go berserk about," Ivor said, making sure that Ronald was out of earshot.

"Do you know, boys, I've had the most splendid idea! Now that you're all having to work for a living, a moneymaking sideline might be to open your house to the public as a haunted house," Lindsey said excitedly.

"Yes, come and see the haunted wardrobe! Ooh," George said, without any hint of sarcasm and doing a feeble impression of a ghost as he spoke.

"Do you know, that's not a bad idea," Ivor said, giving the matter serious consideration. "Of course, in order to capitalise on the wardrobe, we'd have to tell Ronald about it and that would scupper the plan before it even got off the ground."

"You could always lie," Lindsey suggested. "Tell him it's an ordinary wardrobe and that you're working a sting on the plebs."

"Yes! He'd certainly go for that. He's made it his life's work to be a charlatan of the first rank, so if he thinks we're simply pulling a fast one and telling the public we have a possessed wardrobe when we don't, it should work a treat. Do you know, I think we may be on to something here!" Ivor said excitedly.

Rather surprisingly, once back at the house, neither Ivor nor George had long to wait for the first of their deliveries.

"Ah, my furniture," Ivor said, as the first of the delivery men mounted the steps to the door. "If you could take that to my room," he added. "Lindsey, could you show this man where to discharge his load, please?"

"It'll be a pleasure, Ivor," Lindsey said, looking the man up and down.

"Ronald, this looks like some of your stuff," Ivor said, as a bed was brought from the wagon.

"It *is* my bed!" Ronald said.

"How can it be? Your bed was stolen, remember? I've just bought these!" Ivor said, shaking his head dismissively.

"I've been meaning to ask you, Ivor, why didn't we report all our things stolen again?" asked George.

"George, we've been through this. How would it have made us look? 'I'm sorry officer, all our things were stolen whilst we were unconscious on a drugs and cocktails binge'. Yes, that would have been good, wouldn't it?" Ivor answered sarcastically. "If I've said it once, I'll say it again. We have our good name to think of in this town."

How Much for a Shag?

"Oh look, here's my wardrobe," George said, pointing from the window and jumping up and down.

"Right, don't mention it to Ronald. Just make some light small talk!" Ivor said.

"Trust me, Ivor. They don't call me Small-Talking George for nothing!"

"Well, weave some magic, as here he is," Ivor said, quickly turning to the window and whistling as Ronald returned from his bedroom.

"What do you think of that then, Doctor Stumpf?" George asked. "We're taking delivery of a haunted wardrobe and we all know what a nutcase you are about demons and witchcraft and all that."

"What?" Ronald raged, already reaching inside his coat for some hitherto secret weapon.

"George!" Ivor shouted, his face flushing. "What are you talking about?"

"I thought I'd try the old double bluff," George said, leaning over to Ivor so that Ronald wouldn't hear.

"Well double bluff your way out of this!" Ivor said as George felt a light breeze and a *whoosh* sound by his ear. Turning quickly, only to see Ronald wielding a heavy cudgel which he had evidently used to take a swipe at George's head.

"Sorry, Ronald, I was lying. Wardrobe? What's a wardrobe? I don't even know what a wardrobe is! What is a wardrobe, Ivor?" George pleaded as he ran around the room, quickly followed by the self-appointed Witchfinder General.

"Quick, George, the window!" Ivor shouted.

"Yes, Ronald, I meant window, not wardrobe," George shouted. Ronald's swipes continuing unabated.

"It's no good, Ivor. He doesn't seem to like the thought of those either," shrieked George hysterically.

"No, I meant stand in front of the window!" Ivor explained, flinching and flexing as though he was avoiding Ronald's wrath and not George.

"Right you are," said George, coming to an abrupt stop. "He's coming, Ivor, I hope you know what you're doing."

"Trust me," Ivor said.

"He's very fast for a man of his age, you know, Ivor. If you've got a plan, can you get it going please?" George squealed, his voice rising in pitch as the sentence progressed.

"Right and ... move," Ivor said, pushing George just as the wild beast that was Ronald was about to bear down on him. Like an unstoppable force, Ronald could do nothing more than twist his face in a moment's panic before he smashed through the window and landed with a thud in the street below.

"Thank God for that! I thought I was a goner," George said, holding his chest and gasping for breath. "What about Ronald, though? We can't leave him in the street!"

"Oh, balls to him! We'll pick him up later. We'll just tell him he fell from the window whilst looking for patients with pre-existing health problems to flog. He won't be any the wiser. Trust me, I *am* a Doctor," Ivor said, puffing up his chest with pride.

"But what about our good name?" asked George.

"I don't care about his good name. It's only my good name I care about," Ivor said as he pointed in various directions to various workmen.

"Do you know, if I didn't know better, I'd swear we'd bought back all our own furniture," George said.

"Oh, not you as well!" Ivor hissed, acknowledging Lindsey as he arrived back in the front room, his face flushed and sweating.

"That was a big one! We could hardly squeeze it in," he said.

"I'm glad you're back. That gentleman over there with the bulging sack - can you show him where he can empty it?" Ivor asked.

"Oh, I am a busy boy, aren't I," Lindsey said, tripping off to do Ivor's bidding.

"And you needn't think you're getting out of it either, you idle twat. Get over there and show your man where he's to take your wardrobe," Ivor said, pulling George by the ear, then pushing him in the general direction of a large delivery man, groaning under the weight of what didn't look like an especially heavy wardrobe.

"You're going to have to give me a hand with this," the man said. "Either I'm getting old or these things are getting heavier," he added.

"What's in this drawer?" George asked, pointing to a large drawer at the base of the haunted wardrobe. It was a rhetorical question, as he didn't expect the man to know, and even as he asked, he'd begun pulling the handle to find out the answer himself.

"Locked, is it?" asked the man.

"Seems to be. I'd guess that's where the problem is. Who knows what foul, dank things lurk inside," George added, looking at the man as he spoke to see if his words had struck a chord of fear.

"Dirty laundry, you mean? Could be! My underwear tends to get like that in the summer as well," the man said.

It wasn't quite the reply George had anticipated.

How Much for a Shag?

"Something disgusting and unholy from ... the other side. Something neither dead nor alive yet having life."

"Steady on! I don't know what you've heard, but I change my drawers every month whether I need to or not," the man replied indignantly.

If they were going to advertise the house as a haunted house, George thought, then it probably wouldn't be best if he were in charge of marketing and advertising.

I've Just Rolled onto Something Hot and Fleshy

"Right then, get that eyesore out of here," Ivor barked.

"But he's helping me move the wardrobe," George protested.

"I meant the wardrobe, dimwit!" Ivor replied, clapping his hands in an attempt to gee everyone up even though no one was paying him any attention.

"I found these French letters in that sack," Lindsey said, coming back into the room, leafing through a few tattered sheets of paper in his hand.

"So? What do they say?" Ivor asked, only half-interested and not even bothering to look, preferring to keep his attention on the constant stream of furniture entering the house.

"Well, they're all addressed to you," Lindsey said.

"Are they?" Ivor said, his interest piqued.

"Not all from the same person, but definitely all addressed to you."

"Now that is a strange coincidence. Furniture that looks exactly like mine containing letters addressed to me. I'm beginning to think it's not just George's wardrobe that's haunted," Ivor said.

"Ivor, I've been meaning to ask - and please tell me to mind my own business if you think it's nothing to do with me - but why did your father have so much money on him?" Lindsey asked.

"Yes, I was wondering that. He comes to visit for the first time in years then, when I mugged him, he had enough cash on him to buy the town. I can't help thinking it's curious as well. It's almost as if he wanted me to have it," Ivor said, guiding two workmen through the door, although neither paid him the slightest attention.

"Well, to have that much money, he was obviously going to buy something or, at least, pay someone for something," Lindsey added.

"That's the last then," said a ruddy-faced delivery man in the broadest Welsh accent Ivor had ever heard.

"Oh right. Right, you are then," Ivor said, bidding the sorry party goodbye and closing the door. "Where is that useless brother of mine?" he said aloud, directing the question to himself as much as to Lindsey.

Ivor walked briskly to the foot of the stairs and shouted his brother's name. There was no response. Quickly, he mounted the stairs and made his way to George's room, opening the door with a little trepidation.

"George? Oh, you are here. Why didn't you answer me?"

"Sorry Ivor, I was just looking at my new wardrobe. It's great, isn't it? George said, sitting against the wall opposite his new purchase.

"Well it's a pity you've no money left to buy any clothes to go in it," Ivor said, moving around the item and giving it his first proper look.

"Isn't she a beauty?" George said.

"No. To be honest, George, it's the ugliest wardrobe I've ever seen, but as Lindsey suggested, it may make us some money, so I'll let the matter drop for the time being. Start thinking about what you want to say in an advert. If we can get it in the newspaper office before midday tomorrow, it should make the following day's edition. You'd better leave the explaining of it to Ronald to me," Ivor said.

"Righty-ho," George replied, taking a pencil and a sheet of paper from the dressing table Ivor had purchased in his job lot. *Do you enjoy a bang in the middle of the night?* he wrote. *Do your underpants fill when you hear strange noises coming from big cracks? Ever been poked roughly from behind, only to turn and find no one there? Ever awoken, only to find hot breath gasping against your cheek? Then visit Mallard, Stumpf, and Uppham!*, he scrawled, underlining the work as he finished. "There, if that doesn't get them flocking in droves, nothing will!" he said to himself, smiling as he perused his handiwork.

Dashing downstairs, George flung open the door.

"That was quick, George! Still, it's probably good to get this thing perfect before we rouse Ronald. Right then, take it line by line and we'll see what we think," Ivor said, with Lindsey nodding in agreement.

"Right you are. God, this is exciting!" George said. *"Do you enjoy a bang in the middle of the night?"* he began.

"Hmm, I'm not sure *enjoy* is the right word. We're trying to frighten them, remember? How about *Have you ever been awoken in the middle of the night by someone banging away at you?"* Ivor suggested.

"Brilliant," George said, crossing out the original sentence and putting in the amended version.

"Right, next line," Ivor demanded.

"Do your pants fill up when you hear strange noises coming from big cracks?" George read.

"It depends where the crack is. After all, we have to expect these things as we get a little older," Lindsey said.

"No. How about *Do big cracks keep you up all night?"* Ivor suggested.

"God, that's good," George said, jotting Ivor's sentence down. *"Ever been poked roughly from behind, only to turn to find no one there?"* he continued.

"Oh, God! More times than I care to remember!" Lindsey said, flopping back in his seat as if the memory were too much for him.

"Alright, but let's hit them hard with this, George. Let them think that there's a real chance the ghost might get them. How about *Do you want to get poked roughly from behind?*" Ivor suggested.

"You know, you should have written this, Ivor. Your ideas will bring us in a fortune," George said.

"Next," Ivor asked.

"Ever awoken, only to find hot breath gasping against your cheek?" George read.

"Oh, you dear boy! Which cheeks do you mean?" Lindsey queried.

"Not so good, George. I'm thinking *ectoplasm* - how about *Ever had something hot and sticky shoot all over you? Do you fancy some?* Remember, this is the hard sell we're going for," Ivor said. "How's about *Then come and work up a real lather looking at our big box*? Now then, read the whole lot back to me."

"Right, here goes - *Have you ever been awoken in the middle of the night by someone banging away at you? Do big cracks keep you up all night? Do you want to get poked roughly from behind? Ever had something hot and sticky shoot all over you? Do you fancy some? Then come and work up a real lather looking at our big box!"*

"That is brilliant!" Ivor said, jumping to his feet and linking arms with George, the two of them dancing around the room to the imagined sounds of coins chinking in their pockets.

"If that doesn't get them in, nothing will," Lindsey added, also using the occasion as an opportunity to dance, even though he wasn't a part of the money-making scam.

As the dancing stopped and Lindsey could see the two were in an exceptionally good mood, he broached a delicate subject about which he had been biding his time to mention.

"Now that Ronald is out of the way and I have the two of you on your own, there is a certain delicate matter I want to speak to you about."

"Lindsey?" said Ivor, looking confused and furrowing his brow.

"Things haven't been as wonderful for me at my home as I might have had you believe. I've been the victim of a smear campaign. Some blackguard has put it about that my mannerisms are affected."

"That's ridiculous," Ivor said.

"Crazy," echoed George.

"You're both very sweet. Alas, however, I feel I'll have to find somewhere else to live and was wondering - seeing as how this house is so large and you'll now need every penny - whether you'd consider me as a lodger?"

"You can move in as soon as you like. I'm sure your reputation will rise to its former glory once people see you living amongst such educated professionals," Ivorsaid.

"That's great news. Can I move in tonight?" Lindsey asked eagerly.

"We might need your help in getting Ronald in first. He is still lying in the road, isn't he?" Ivor said, moving to the window. "Ah, look at him there! Sleeping like a baby!"

"Right, shall we do it?" said George.

"We better had," Ivor replied, moving to the front door.

Within a moment or two, all three men were standing over Ronald's prone body.

"Remember, mind! Don't mention the wardrobe!" Ivor said, leaning over Ronald and giving him a few slaps across the face.

"He's not looking too good, Ivor," George said.

"No, but then he never did. Only two things will wake him – hearing someone say his name and the mention of money! Stand back, I'm going to see if this works," Ivor said. "Doctor Stumpf, your son-in-law, Gerald, is here. He has the money you stole from your charity for you but has said that given you're unconscious he'll spend it on himself."

Suddenly, Ronald went into convulsions and began coughing, his eyes beginning to roll.

"Hey, it's worked!" George said as Ronald sat bolt upright as though in shock.

"Now don't worry, Ronald, you've had a little accident, that's all," Ivor said in his best bedside manner.

"Oh, no, these are the only pair of drawers I've got," Ronald said, shaking his head as though trying to free himself from a daze.

"No, not that sort of accident this time. No, you were leaning from the window looking for some children to whip when you slipped and fell. You've been out cold for a while, so we'd better get you inside," Ivor said, nodding to George and Lindsey that it was now safe to approach. "It's like I said to you before, Ronald - go for the sick and injured ones first!"

"They can't get away so fast," George advised.

"Well, if you don't need me, I'll just be off," Lindsey said. Unfortunately, turning his back on Ronald and moving quickly away proved a mistake, as Stumpf sprang into action, unleashing his bullwhip and catching Lindsey on the back of his legs.

"Ooh, there's a man who knows what he likes!" said Lindsey, dusting himself down as Ivor and George did their best to restrain the old huckster.

"Quick! Go now!" Ivor said. "We'll deal with Ronald."

Within a few brief moments, Ronald had been taken back into the house and lain on a sofa to recuperate.

"Now Ronald, you know we've been put in a situation where we have to try and get some money. We've been having a bit of a think around the problem and have come up with the idea of doing some guided tours around the place, advertising it as a haunted house. We all know it isn't - God forbid that we should be messing around with the dark side, us all being devout Christians - but it seems like a pretty good way of getting the plebs to part with their money. What do you think?" Ivor said.

Ronald pulled a face that he imagined made him look implacably determined.

"It's just another scam, Ronald, just like the good old days. Money for old rope!" Ivor enforced.

"I don't know. He who sups with the Devil should have a long spoon," Ronald said.

"Ronald, it's not like that. We're *pretending* the house is haunted for hard cash. That's the end of it.

You must be able to see that that's easy money?" Ivor coerced.

"You might even get to flog a few stragglers!" George said as an aside, unaware of how strong a selling point money and cruelty would be to the old mountebank.

"Tremendous! I think this sounds like an unbelievable business idea!" Ronald said, stroking his chin. "And *nobody* knows more about business than me!"

"I'd also like your opinion on our getting a lodger as it will be easy money," Ivor asked.

"Easy money? That's tremendous! Really beautiful! Unbelievable!" Ronald replied.

"Phew, that's settled then," Ivor said, rubbing his hands in glee.

"Shall I read Ronald our advert?" George asked.

"Now that would be a good idea. I think it's important that Ronald understands the sort of customers we're targeting."

"Right, here goes! *Have you ever been awoken in the middle of the night by someone banging away at you? Do big cracks keep you up all night? Do you want to get poked roughly from behind? Ever had something hot and sticky shoot all over you? Do you fancy some? Then come and work up a real lather looking at our big box*," George read excitedly.

"Well, what do you think?" Ivor asked, looking at Ronald, who seemed to be thinking about what he'd just heard.

"Unbelievable! Really great! This is going to be tremendous! *Nobody* knows more about haunted houses than me!" he said, giving a thumbs-up gesture.

"Anything you'd like to change?" Ivor asked.

"My drawers," Stumpf replied.

"No, about the advert," Ivor said, now used to Stumpf not following conversations unless they were about himself.

"More sex!"

"Well, we hadn't thought of putting any on. Maybe we could get George in a dress but it wasn't top of the agenda. Do you think we need to sell that angle to make it a success?" Ivor asked.

"Definitely! *Nobody* knows more about sex than me!"

"Right, George, you can show the people round in a dress!" Ivor said.

"Right you are!" George replied, confusing 'in a dress' with 'the address', and feeling rather important that he had suddenly been promoted to the chief tour guide.

Sometime later, there came a noise from the street.

"That sounds like Lindsey," Ivor said, as a voice from the street shouted a cheery 'Yoo-hoo' and a few taps rapped out on the door.

"That was quick," remarked George as he swung open the door, only to see Lindsey on the top step with an array of furniture removers behind him.

"Yes, I like my men to be fast," said Lindsey, ushering his entourage inside. "Be careful with my Saint Sebastian as it's very precious to me," he said to one burly youth manhandling a picture of the tortured martyr.

"Very nice," said George, nodding at the painting.

"Right, if I can have all the Gothic on this side of the room and all the Neo-Classicism on this side," Lindsey said, clapping his hands to capture the workmen's attention, then watching as they milled about in abject confusion.

"Perhaps you ought to let me handle this, Lindsey," Ivor said. "I know how the peasantry thinks," he began before one of the delivery men interrupted.

"Right, if you could all look at the artefact you're holding and appraise it for dominance of form over content, technical precision over an expressiveness torn from one's soul, artistic restraint, clarity of style over the free play of one's imagination and the ambiguous extravagance that some seem to think the latest thing," he explained, as Mallard, Stumpf, and Uppham gazed at each other in mute confusion. "I can see that you're obviously making a critical assessment," the delivery man continued, now addressing his remarks to the three Doctors.

"Will you rotten shower get it upstairs!" Ronald shouted.

"Ivor! I hadn't realised you'd employed such an aesthete," Lindsey said joyously, clasping his hands together and broadly smiling.

"Well, yes. I've always been a keen sportsman you know. I used to do a fair bit of boxing and rowing when I was younger so wanted someone fit enough to lift things," Ivor said, shuffling uneasily.

"God, Ivor, and I thought I was thick! You're thinking of *athlete*. Lindsey meant one of those little white parrot things, didn't you Lindsey?" George said. Lindsey, however, had already lost interest and was busy ensuring none of his precious artefacts had been broken under Ronald's onslaught.

Surprisingly, once all Lindsey's possessions had been taken to his room, he managed to get them arranged quite quickly into a style with which he could live.

As night drew on, George became ever more excited about what might be unleashed from his wardrobe. It was only after everyone had retired for the night, exhausted by the frantic pace of the day, that George was finally able to set his mind to nothing else.

After he had been lying in repose for thirty or so minutes a gentle knock came at his door startling him as he sought to locate the sound, thinking it may have come from his new acquisition.

"George, I've found this old dress amongst some of the things delivered today. I know it's not your colour and it won't do you justice, but I know how difficult it can be to get used to the fabric against your skin," Ivor said, tossing the dress George's way as he turned to inspect the wardrobe.

"Eh? Nobody said I'd have to wear a dress! Why have I got to wear a dress?" George said, rubbing his eyes, half hoping he had been imagining his brother's request.

"We did, downstairs, don't you remember? You agreed to it after Ronald said the public wants sex," Ivor said.

"Eh?" George grunted, beginning to feel more and more alarmed.

"Just put the dress on and tell me how it feels," Ivor said sharply.

As George slid into the dress, his initial hesitation left him and he began to walk up and down the room, enjoying the flow of the fabric. Suddenly, however, there came a loud tearing noise and an awful smell permeated the room.

"Don't look at me like that! It wasn't me," Ivor said, holding his nose.

"Well, it wasn't me either. Ladies don't do that sort of thing!" George replied.

Then came a terrible groaning and a slow rhythmic tapping that gradually got faster then suddenly stopped.

"Ronald reading *Fanny Hill*, again?" George suggested.

"No, the groaning wasn't loud enough," Ivor said dismissively, craning his neck to locate the sound's origin.

"Ivor, look!" George said, staring fearfully at the wardrobe, which had begun shaking from side to side.

"Oh, God!" Ivor shouted, running from the room as quickly as he could, back to his room and sanctuary. Shutting the door behind him, he leapt for his bed before pulling the sheets back and diving under the covers, quickly pulling them up and over his head. No sooner had he done so, than they were torn forcibly from his grip.

"Go away! It's not me you want! It's George! It was his idea to sell you as a cheap sideshow. It was him that bought you," Ivor said, his eyes screwed up in terror.

"Ivor, it's me! I'm coming in! I'm frightened," George said shaking, clambering into the bed before he'd even had an answer.

"Shh, be quiet! I think I can hear something," Ivor said as the two of them lay panting as quietly as they could, straining to hear the slightest creak.

"God! There it was again!" George said.

"Oh, God! This is all your fault! If you hadn't bought that damn thing in the first place, none of this would have happened. Ronald was right! We are messing with the forces of darkness. Oh, God! Oh, God!" Ivor whimpered. Suddenly there was a loud bang as if the wardrobe had fallen over.

"I'm off to Ronald's room. He'll know what to do," Ivor said, running desperately to the door and flinging it open.

"Well if you're going, so am I. You're not leaving me here on my own, you swine! That's what you want, isn't it? To come back in the morning and find the shrivelled husk of your brother with all his juices having been sucked out," George said, leaping from the bed and grabbing hold of Ivor's arm.

Ivor sprinted across the hall and pushed open Ronald's door, pulling George into the room behind him before slamming it shut.

"I'm coming in with you, Doctor Stumpf," George explained, tearing back Ronald's sheets and diving under cover

"So am I! Something is going on out there," Ivor said, following his brother's lead.

"I heard something as well. I thought it was one of you two!"

"Ronald, I think it's a ghost!" said Ivor.

"Shut up, will you?" George said, pulling the sheet above his head.

"Don't tell me to shut up," Ivor said, reaching over to slap his brother.

"Don't or I'll ... uh ... oh, God! I've just rolled onto something hot and fleshy," George said.

"Oh, God, don't say that! It's him, he's got his hand in the bed," Ivor said, flailing his arms wildly.

"No, it's mine!" Ronald said.

"Well can you keep your hands to yourself, please!" George said indignantly. "I didn't come into this bed to get groped!"

"It's not my hand, dimwit!" Ronald replied.

"Oh, God, that's even worse! Ivor, can you tell him!" George said in disgust.

"Look!" Ronald said, pulling back the sheets. "It's the last of my sausages. I felt hungry, so I made myself

217

a late snack. I was eating them when you two burst in," he explained. "Oh, God, pull your nightshirt back down, can you?" Ronald said, turning to Ivor and noting that his wild thrashing had caused his nightshirt to ride up above his waist.

"Shh! What's that?" George said, freezing in terror.

As he spoke, footsteps could be heard on the landing outside. Moving from bedroom to bedroom, something was opening each door in turn.

"He's looking for us! It knows where we are and is looking for us! This is all your fault!" Ivor said, reaching across Ronald and grabbing his brother by the throat.

"Oh, God, look!" said Ronald, pointing with his sausage.

As the three Doctors looked, even in the dim orange glow of Ronald's oil lamp, the handle of the door could be seen twisting, its various bumps and dents throwing off reflections that made it scintillate.

The door swung open and there, silhouetted against the landing light, was Lindsey.

"Oh, my boys! My beautiful, beautiful boys!" said Lindsey, gazing rapturously at the scene before him. There, in the small bed, lay George, his lithe body clad in a flimsy dress stained with squashed sausage; Ivor, his nightshirt high above his waist, exposing all his lower half, his hands wrapped tightly around George's throat; and Ronald, pointing at the door with the firmest sausage Lindsey had ever seen.

"I had no idea. I'd never have interrupted, had I known," Lindsey."

"Lindsey, this is not what it looks like," Ivor began.

"No! After Ivor got me into a dress, the groaning and banging got too loud in my room so we sneaked into his. From there, we came to Ronald's room, hoping he'd give us the benefit of his experience, not realising he was busy with his sausage. Then, when we heard you coming, we didn't know what to do," George added.

"Don't worry, George. We're all men of the world. I'm sure you weren't up to anything I haven't seen many times before," Lindsey said, his eyes twinkling.

"Yes, George, you're not helping," Ivor said, pulling his nightshirt down as Ronald took a bite of his sausage.

"No, I heard a knocking and a deep, heavy groaning. I thought I'd better investigate, but I think the mystery's been solved," Lindsey said, bowing courteously as he bade farewell.

"No, wait, Lindsey," Ivor said.

"Yes, Ivor?" Lindsey replied, eagerly jumping back into the room.

"We heard the banging and groaning too."

"Well, I hope you don't think it was me!" Lindsey said indignantly.

"No! We know what the noise is and where it came from, that's the problem. It's from that wretched wardrobe that George bought," Ivor explained.

"The haunt ... the hau ... the war ... the walnut one?" Lindsey stammered, remembering halfway through that the word 'haunted' was never to be used in earnest in Doctor Stumpf's company.

"That's the one," confirmed Ivor. "Well, now that we're all together, perhaps we ought to go and take a look at this wardrobe. You know, safety in numbers and all that."

"I'm game," said Lindsey.

"I suppose," George said uneasily.

"Ronald?" Ivor asked.

"Let me just finish my sausage and I'll be with you."

Queenie Will Turn a Few Tricks for You

"Right you are. Let's be off," Ronald said, swallowing the last of his sausage.

"I'm nervous," George said, grabbing hold of Ivor's arm when he wasn't looking, causing him to leap in the air.

"Will you stop that! If it hadn't been for you in the first place, none of this would have happened," Ivor hissed.

"Shh!" Ronald sounded, as he drew near the door. "Well, I can't hear a thing," he said as he twisted the handle and entered the room.

The other three followed, all the while gearing themselves up to flee at a moment's notice.

"It looks the same," George said, moving about the room, then towards the wardrobe, sniffing carefully in the thought that it was somehow the safest means of contact.

"What's in the drawer?" Ronald said, bending down and pulling the drawer handle until his face went a burnt orange. "Ah, it must be a fake one," he concluded.

"Well, that's that then, isn't it?" Ivor said, brushing his hands and trying to regain control. "It was all in George's imagination! It's a good thing I was here to put his mind at rest."

"And yours! You imagined it too!" George bleated.

"Now, perhaps we can all get some sleep?" Ivor suggested, brushing George's comments to one side. "I'm hoping for a busy day tomorrow. Our advert should be out and I'm expecting quite a crowd."

Ivor, Ronald and Lindsey slowly filed out of the room, leaving George alone. George walked around the wardrobe and nervously touched it a few times. He hadn't imagined anything, he knew that. Now, the whole room felt as though an awful presence was in it. George slowly pulled the dress up to his shoulders then, as quickly as he could, pulled it over his head, lest the ghost, beast, or whatever it was, struck him in that brief second when he wasn't looking. It might have been the Age of Reason, but it didn't cost anything to take such things for granted!

He climbed into bed, a difficult task given he was loathe to take his eyes off the wardrobe for even an instant. As soon as he was in bed, he pulled the sheets over his head. No! That was worse. Now *it* knew he couldn't see what things it was up to and had come out into the bedroom and was waiting for him to pull back the sheets!

Then it would strike! What cruelties! Why wouldn't it just finish him off now, when he couldn't see? Why wait until he had torn back the sheets, only to stare into its demonic eyes? Because it thrived on his fear, that's why!

This was unbearable! He couldn't spend all night cowering under the covers whilst the thing filled the room about him with its huge slimy presence, waiting in cold satisfaction! No, he would tear back the sheets and fight! That was the thing to do! George pulled back the sheets and flailed his arms about him, his eyes screwed up in abject terror - for these things had a tendency to go for the eyes - that much he knew!

When George opened his eyes, he was surprised to find the room as quiet as it had been when first he had gone to bed. It must have read his mind, and knowing he was about to pull the sheets back, leapt back into the wardrobe! That was worse! Now it could read his mind, so there could be no escape, for it knew what he was about to do before he did it!

George propped himself up against the headboard with his pillows and, being undecided as to whether one was safer from such things with one's head under or over the sheets, concluding that the safest course of action would be to pull the sheets up to a level just below the eyes. Now he could see what was going on in the room and feel halfway protected by the sheets.

It wasn't until the first rays of the morning sun began to enter the room that George allowed himself a little sleep, what with monsters being nocturnal beasts. Now he had the safety of daylight on his side, no monster could get him!

By the time Lindsey knocked on his door at around nine that morning, George had had just a few hours' sleep.

"Hello George," Lindsey said. "I've brought you a cup of tea after your fright last night. My heart went out to you, it really did! I haven't seen anyone shudder so much since I was an undergraduate at Oxford and the young Montague Ryley-Gould had a touch of the vapours when performing in Apuleius' *Golden Ass*."

"Thank you, Lindsey," George said, rubbing his tired eyes and taking the tea.

"I think this might be a busy day," Lindsey continued, as he pulled back George's curtains. "Ivor's already gone to the shops to get you a few new frocks. We need to have you looking your best, don't we? As much as I like scarlet, I don't think it shows off those eyes of yours. A nice emerald green or a bright blue is what you want."

"Good. I can't wear the dress I wore last night again until it's clean," George said, yawning and stretching

"Is it dirty?" Lindsey asked, sitting himself down on the edge of George's bed.

"Yes, I got this dreadful mark down the back of it from Ronald."

"I *knew* something was going on last night! I must say, he's a game old bird, isn't he?" Lindsey laughed.

"No, you don't understand. It's stained with juice from Ronald's sausage," George explained.

"You don't need to explain to me," Lindsey said. "It's us against them in this world, George."

"Anyway, the advert goes out today," George said, taking a sip of tea and trying to change the subject.

"Oh, I'd forgotten that," Lindsey replied, then paused for a moment or two. "Oh, don't say there's some dreadfully boring reason Ivor's buying those dresses," he said in disappointment.

"That's the only reason!" George answered, half choking on his tea.

"Oh, how dreary. I hadn't realised business came before pleasure," Lindsey replied wistfully.

"And what's your role in this new venture?" George asked.

"I don't think I've been accorded anything yet. Ivor said he's going to slip me in wherever he can."

"I suppose I'd better be getting up," George said. "Uh ... out of bed, I mean."

"Then I'll leave you to it," Lindsey said, leaving George to prepare for the trials of the day.

George dressed quickly. As he descended the stairs, Ivor opened a door.

"Ah, George! I'm glad you're up. I've some frocks for you to put on."

"Do I have to?" George answered, pulling a face.

"It's money in the bank, George," Ivor replied.

With some reluctance, George removed his masculine apparel and pulled over his head the first dress from the pile - a bright blue muslin number with a double-breasted bodice and the skirt cut away at the front to reveal a full muslin petticoat.

"Don't forget this!" Ivor said, gathering a long muslin scarf around George's shoulders, crossing it over his chest and securing it in his waist ribbon. "There, how do you feel?"

"Like a princess!" George said. "I could dance my life away."

"I'll dance with you," Lindsey said, leaping to his feet and taking George in his arms. "Oh, the Waltz! Queen of all the Dances! What was it Goethe said? *Never have I moved so lightly. I was no longer a human being. To hold the most adorable creature in one's arms and fly around with her like the wind, so that everything around us fades away,"* he said, closing his eyes as he whirled George around the room.

"So ... uh ... you think you'll be able to get used to wearing a dress then, George?" Ivor asked nervously. "Right, I'll tell the dressmaker we'll take that one, shall I?" he added when his first sentence was ignored, only to find his second was also ignored.

"Sorry Ivor, you were saying something?" George asked.

"Yes, I was asking if that's the one," Ivor said.

"Oh yes. I've never danced with anyone so light on their feet," George said, smiling at Lindsey, who bowed and blushed.

"No, the dress, you dimwit! You're supposed to be a sexy vamp, not some queen of the ball swanning around the place. Remember what Ronald's sister used to say? 'Sex sells!'"

While Ivor went back to the dress shop to take back the other dresses and pay for the one George had chosen, George changed back into his frock coat and britches.

"Do you know if Ivor's thought of any itinerary, or are we going to play it by ear?" George asked, sitting down to breakfast and directing his question at Lindsey who sat on a sofa at the other end of the room.

"He did say something about writing something down, but I don't think he's got around to it. I know he's had a poster printed up to advertise though. He's putting it in a few shop windows," Lindsey replied.

"So, what is Ivor's role in all of this?" George asked with concerned curiosity.

"He says he's coordinating."

"I see. Sitting on his backside doing nothing and getting paid for doing it, in other words," George replied.

Within a few minutes, Ivor was back, looking flushed and excited.

"It's happening! I can't believe the interest my leaflet has created. George, get your dress on. You're giving your first guided tour at ten this morning," Ivor said, running around like a dervish.

"Hang on a minute! What do I say? Who's coming?" George asked, almost choking on his toast.

"Does it matter? I think about half a dozen people are coming. Just make it up as you go along. For God's sake, just use some imagination, it can't be that difficult," Ivor said abruptly.

As George finished the last of his breakfast and pulled on his dress, there was a knock at the door. Ivor answered.

"We've come about the advert," said a gaunt, elderly man, a little out of date in that he still wore a wig, albeit unpowdered and tied at the back with a black ribbon.

"Yes. If you could just purchase some tickets from our ticket vendor," Ivor said, ushering the group towards Lindsey, who looked around the room for the newly appointed vendor until he realised Ivor had been pointing at him.

"Right, if you could all bear with me. I'm quite new to this game - God, it's been years since I last said anything like that! - but I'm afraid I don't have any tickets at the moment. I can gladly take your money and Queenie over there will turn a few tricks for you, although I can also put my hand to anything if the price is right," Lindsey said, taking the cash and pointing at George.

"Yes, thank you, Mr Grayson," George said. "As my colleague mentioned, my name is Queenie," he said, casting a long, dirty look in Lindsey's direction. "Queenie Uppham and I'm your tour guide this morning. If you'd all like to follow me."

With that, the little troupe walked from the main room to a dining room that had once doubled as a surgery.

"In here, strange and terrible things are said to have happened," George began, once the group had drawn around him. "Even now, if you listen very carefully, you may hear a terrible groaning," he added, anticipating that Ronald's snoring would be resonating through the house. As if by clockwork, the snore came, causing a little hubbub amongst the group. "It is a known fact that in this room many people have met painful deaths," George said, remembering the time he and Ivor had tried to cure baldness by offering head transplants.

"Right, please follow me," George continued, ushering the group from the room and catching the eyes of an old lecher, who brought up the rear of the group, for the first time.

George made his way down a passage, towards the door that led to his cowshed-cum-laboratory.

"Here, we have a cowshed," he began. "You will notice the strange, unholy smell in this room," he began, pointing out the cowpats and human viscera as he spoke."Dear God, what a smell!" said a voice from the back.

"Yes, perhaps we won't linger in this room too long," George said gesturing, right and left, at nothing in particular as he wafted from the room. "Right, if we mount these stairs, we shall now see some more rooms in which many a terrifying presence has been felt."

George came to Ivor's surgery and gave the doorknob a turn. As he opened the door, Ivor was revealed there naked, rubbing his body with the money they had just taken.

"Uh, perhaps we won't go in there," George said, quickly slamming the door as he saw the scene and the look of horror shooting across Ivor's face.

"I want you, you honey-hipped strumpet," said the elderly man quietly, and out of earshot of the others, pressing himself up against George.

"Let's move on," George said, grinding his heel into the man's little toe, whilst glancing back in the hope that he had stolen one of Ronald's sausages and that it had been that that had been pressed so firmly against him. "Here, we come to one of the most evil rooms in the house. Even I have had a terrible experience in this room. Why, just last night I rolled over and felt something hot and fleshy pressing against my back," he confessed, catching the old man's eye as he spoke, only to see him lecherously flicking his tongue and winking.

George opened the door to Ronald's room and waited a moment to allow the unforgiving stench to seep out, watching as it coiled its way up the legs of the visitors like ghostly vines.

"Here you will see the late Doctor Ronald Stumpf," George said, pointing at Ronald asleep in the bed.

"But he's breathing," said a voice.

"And snoring!" came a second.

"And flatulating!" came a third as a terrible sound echoed around the room, giving the distinct impression that Ronald had somehow torn the sheets in two without moving a muscle.

"Yes, many people have remarked on his near lifelike appearance. Not only that, but his body also refuses to decay ..."

"Well, it doesn't smell like it!" said the elderly man, holding his nose.

"But his flesh remains incorruptible. Many have said that dark forces are at work and, should his body ever arise again, he will wreak havoc and destruction on those who have
disturbed his eternal repose," George said, warming to his task at last.

As the group made to leave, George lingered back, knowing full well the old man would follow suit.

"Look," George said, pushing the old man toward Ronald's bed, tripping him up as he did so, and slamming the door loudly enough to wake the sleeping Doctor. From the cries and desperate scrapings on the other side of the door, George knew the old lecher had been dealt with in no uncertain terms.

"Where's my father?" said one of the all-male group as George re-joined them.

"Oh, he found that last room so fascinating he asked if he could stay on and be given a real going-over ... sorry, give it a real going-over," George replied, stammering so much he almost gave the game away. He quickly pushed his way to the front of the group, avoiding eye contact with the three remaining men, all of whom were either arching eyebrows, preening sideburns, or running their fingers through their hair. Ivor had been right! Sex was selling!

"And now we come to the climax of this morning's entertainment," George said, opening the door to his room. "Gentlemen, I give you the haunted wardrobe!"

There was not the merest hint of a response as the attendant faces looked back expressionless.

"The haunted wardrobe!" George said again, trying to give his act a little pizzazz by gesturing to the wardrobe with both arms and a big smile on his face.

"And?" asked one of the men, as if there should be something else.

"What do you mean *and*? What do you want it to do? It's a wardrobe and it's haunted. It can't, therefore, be anything other than a haunted wardrobe, can it?" George said indignantly.

"So, does the man come out of there?" asked the second tourist.

"Ah, we don't know it's a man. It could be a woman!" George said, taking a step back as the word 'woman' raised a cheer amongst the group. "Or even a beast!" he added, again taking a step backwards in surprise as an even louder cheer erupted.

"So, what time does the show start?" said one of the men, sitting on the edge of George's bed.

"What time does the show start? It's finished! The show is over!" George said, shaking his head in confusion.

"Have we missed it then?" said the second man.

"Missed it? You just had it!" George replied.

"Look, let's not beat about the bush. We've come to see a sex show and we want to know what time it starts," the man on the edge of the bed explained.

"A sex show! No, I'm afraid this is a haunted house. There's never been any sex here," George blushed.

"Look, your advert asked if we wanted to see someone getting *poked from behind* and then get *something hot and sticky shot all over them*," the third man said aggressively.

"And it also said you had someone here with a *big box*!" said the man on the bed.

"No, you've misunderstood! We were trying to make the advert sound sexy. That's why I'm in a dress. You'd never usually find me in a dress," said George

"I say, it's pretty liberated!" said the first man, arching his eyebrow and gazing at George in mistaken longing as the other two cheered.

"We've paid for a sex show!" said the second man.

"And that is what we'll get," the third man said, pulling a small pistol from his boot.

"Oh, *the* sex show! Right, I'll just go and see if they're ready," George said uneasily, making his way to the door.

Quickly, George plunged down the stairs and burst in on Ivor, who by now had dressed and had begun counting the money instead of rubbing himself with it.

"They want a sex show!" George said breathlessly.

"What! Not in my house! Wait ... how much did they offer you?" Ivor asked.

"Not with me! They want to watch one. They think we're going to put on a performance!" George explained.

"What! My God, George, what have you been saying to these people? I said 'sex sells', but I didn't expect you to say we'd throw in an erotic floorshow," Ivor shouted.

"No, it was the advert. They say they were misled and that they didn't come here to see a haunted house at all. When I said that there wasn't a sex show one of them pulled a gun out on me and threatened to kill me unless they had their show," he stammered.

"And is his shooter loaded?" Ivor asked.

"Yes, it's in his hand as we speak!"

"And the gun?"

"Yes, that as well," answered George.

"We need to think fast," Ivor said, pacing the room and looking at the floor. "I have it," he snapped. "I'll go into town and buy three false beards."

"Ivor, we're in trouble! This is no time for a fancy-dress party!"

"No, dimwit. We'll give them some crap story about having to wear beards before they can see the show. Then, when they've got the beards on, we give Ronald a *Knee Trembler* and tell him Clivella has returned with her sisters and that they all want a piece of his wrinkled old arse."

"I don't get it," said George.

"Well, he's going to go in there in a frenzy, isn't he? Can you imagine the scene when all three spurn his advances? God, it'll be like The French Revolution!" Ivor reasoned.

"Ivor, that is the work of a genius! No wonder you've scaled the heights with such a cunning mind," George replied, slapping his brother across the back.

"Right, you get Ronald, I'll get the beards and we'll see if Lindsey can give us a *Kiss Behind the Cowshed*," Ivor said, dashing from the room.

George followed as quickly as he could, then made his way to Ronald's room, instead of downstairs after Ivor.

"No, I meant the drink, you idiot," Ivor's voice bellowed up the stairs before the back door slammed shut.

"Doctor Stumpf?" George said quietly, tapping at Ronald's door as lightly as he could. He braced himself as he heard heavy footsteps approaching from the other side and the noise of the knob turning.

"Yes?" Ronald said.

"I think Ivor wants to tell you something. I believe it's rather urgent," George said.

"Of course! No problem," Ronald said cheerily.

"You seem in good spirits this morning, Doctor Stumpf," George ventured.

"Yes. I just met someone that was in my year in school. There was no laughing at 'Stumpf's stump' today, that's for sure! Not so brave without Donkey Davis or Plums Price to back him up!" Ronald said wistfully.

"Then I think this is your lucky day. If I'm not mistaken, Ivor's got some very good news for you."

As they descended the stairs together, the front door burst open with a fearful noise.

"Excuse me, Doctor Stumpf," George said. "I'm a bit nervous," he added, just as Ivor returned with the false beards, beckoning George to one side.

"Here you are. Get them upstairs and onto the faces of those parasites as quickly as possible," he said.

"Blonde? Clivella's hair was as black as it coal," George said.

"Look, it was the best I could do at short notice, alright? Anyway, Ronald likes blondes and after Lindsey gives him a *Knee Trembler*, I don't think he'll care what colour it is so long as it's warm and hairy."

As fast as he could, George ascended the stairs and ran straight to his room.

"Uh, gentlemen. I have a somewhat strange request. You are, indeed, about to encounter an experience you will never forget. Our show, however, is an interactive experience in which you - our audience - will be called upon to join in the fun! In order, therefore, to protect your anonymity - and to give you something with which to tickle our performers! - we're supplying you with these beards. If you could keep them on at all times, the management would be very grateful," George said.

Then, as if on cue, an enormous drunken bellow came thundering up the stairs and the door to George's room burst open.

"Quick, George, get out while you can!" Ivor shouted, tugging George by the sleeve of his dress and pulling him from the room just a second before Doctor Stumpf entered, slamming the door firmly behind him.

"Old Ronald will give them a sex show they won't forget, won't he!" George laughed

"Well, they'll certainly get some sex, and it will certainly be a show, but I don't think the experience will be a completely erotic one!" Ivor said, as the door burst open and three men in beards sped past, fleeing for their lives.

"Thank you. Come again!" George shouted after them, laughing with hysterical relief.

"Hello boys," came a loud voice, unexpectedly interrupting the premature celebration.

"I know that voice," Ivor said, squinting into the room.

"So do I. Now don't tell me!" George said. "It's Eldritch!"

"Fancy a song, lads? I've got my mattock - or tuning fork if you prefer! This is a particular favourite of mine and is in the key of B flat," he said, taking a well-aimed swipe at Ivor and George. "What do you know? Two birds with one stone," he said, congratulating himself, as the two Doctors tumbled to the floor. "Be flat. Get it? Oh well. Please yourselves."

Fancy a Quickie?

"Oh, God, my head hurts," Ivor said, rubbing the back of his neck and moving his head around in the vain hope that one position might be more comfortable than another.

"Mine too," said George, pushing his closed eyes around in their sockets.

"What were we drinking, for God's sake?" Ivor asked.

"I don't think we were, were we? I think I'd know if I'd had a *Quickie* after a *Kiss Behind the Cowshed* and I don't feel as though I've had either," George replied, opening his eyes. "Oh, God, now I remember," he added, nudging Ivor with his elbow.

"What is it? Can't you leave me alone? You can see that I'm ill and you're still keeping on!" Ivor moaned.

"No, it's not that. I remember why we feel so bad, and it's nothing to do with the drink. It's Eldritch!" said George, looking at Eldritch lying on George's bed, as he watched them regain consciousness on the floor opposite.

"Oh please, George! Don't even mention that fat fugger's name, even in jest. The thought of him coming back sends a shiver down my back," Ivor replied, giving an involuntary shudder.

"Oh, it does, does it?" Eldritch said indignantly.

"Stop it, George! I know you're good at impressions, but I don't want you doing him. God, for a moment there I thought he was actually in the room with us," Ivor said, finally opening his eyes. "Ah, Eldritch. How strange that you should be here just as George and I were talking about another Eldritch we know. Do you know him? He's an awful man!" Ivor stammered nervously.

"Don't give me that balls, Mallard! I know you were talking about me," Eldritch scowled.

"Nonsense! We like you, don't we, George?"

"Yes. In fact, I think I'm falling in love with him," said George, straightening his dress.

"Eh?" said Eldritch, a look of shock on his face.

"Don't overdo it, halfwit," Ivor hissed. "No, what George meant is that he loves you like a brother. You're almost family to him," Ivor explained.

"Yes, that's what I meant. Sorry," George said, abashed.

"It's alright boys. I know I'm not a well-liked man," Eldritch admitted.

"That's rubbish! I don't know anyone who's as popular as you!" Ivor said. "Alright, so a few people in the town might have objected to you digging up their relatives and selling them, but what they don't understand is that a man has to make a living," he added.

"Exactly!" Eldritch agreed, moving to the edge of the bed, beginning to involve himself in the conversation

"I mean to say, how else are you going to pay for gin and filthy woodcuts?" George ventured.

Before Eldritch could answer, there came a groaning from the wardrobe.

"See, it's the ghost! It's back again!" George said nervously.

"Ghost? No, that's that old Doctor friend of yours. I locked him in the wardrobe after he tried to kiss me. I couldn't believe it! Running his fingers through my beard, he was, and telling me I was the most beautiful woman he'd ever seen and how he liked his women carrying a bit of baggage as it gave him something to hold on to when the action started," Eldritch said in disbelief.

"Yes, that sounds like Stumpf alright. He must have mistaken you for his last girlfriend," explained Ivor.

"Anyway, I hit him with the mattock and put him in that drawer I was in before," said Eldritch.

"Oh, so it was you! God, that's a relief. I thought it was a ghost!" laughed George.

"No! Listen, boys, I do have a bit of a confession to make. You're probably wondering why I was in your wardrobe drawer, to begin with, eh?" he said.

"If you want to climb into our drawers, Mr Eldritch, then I can't begin to tell you how happy I am about it," Ivor grovelled.

"My drawers are always open to you ... uh, in a manner of speaking," George stammered.

"Well, anyway. I went into a little business venture with a few people. They wanted you lot out of this house. I thought to myself I could come around here and throw you out, but that would have caused too many arguments and I don't like upset. The other idea was to come around and slit your throats, but then I'd have all those bodies to get rid of and seeing as how you lot are my best customers, it'd be like slitting my own throat, so to speak - or biting the hand that feeds you if, you prefer. So, anyway, Nelly suggested to me that we wait until you had a drink one night and we'd be able to clean you out, seeing as how Ivor would be the first to pass out and the others would quickly follow. With you all unconscious, we could take away all your things and then, given you'd have no means of making a living, you'd not be able to stay living in the house and would move out of your own accord. I'd get the job done with no mess, a few bob from the furniture and a few bob from that Uppham bloke for getting him the house," Eldritch said.

"I won't stand for that! Where did this vicious rumour start that it's always me that's the first to pass out? What about George? One good ... hang on a minute! Did you say that a man named Uppham was paying you to get rid of us?" Ivor asked.

"Yes. He should have been here a few days ago with the cash. I know why as well! He was intending to buy up all the houses in the street as there's an underground stream running beneath these houses and it's got a rich vein of gold in it."

"Swine! His own children! He was quite prepared to have seen you kill us both, just to get his hands on some gold in a stream?" Ivor ranted.

"Don't take it so personally. Worse things happen at sea," Eldritch said sympathetically.

Once again, a loud groaning came from the wardrobe.

"Shut up, you old git," Eldritch shouted, banging the wardrobe with his mattock.

"So how did you come to be in the wardrobe?" George asked.

"That's where it all went wrong. You remember I'd been enjoying the company of Nelly," Eldritch began. "Well, when I came out and met that friend of yours we got into a little tussle, during which he threw me from that window, and I'll admit I was dazed for a while and didn't know what to do. Then, Nelly comes out and says the coast was all clear, as you'd all been drinking and we could now clean you out. That took us a good few hours. Then, as I was waiting outside loading up the last wagon, that hairy boyfriend of Doctor Stumpf's knocks me on the head. Next thing I knew, I was waking up in the wardrobe. I suppose you must have bought it by then, as once I managed to get the thing open, I was here."

"God, it's amazing isn't it?" George remarked.

"What?" said Eldritch, wondering which part of his story George had found so astonishing.

"How God made the world in six days. God, it takes me that long just to get my clothes clean after a night out!" George remarked, looking vacantly into the distance. "God, he's great, isn't he!"

"Who?" asked Ivor, confused as to where George was taking his new strand of conversation.

"God, of course! Imagine being God! 'You've been a bad boy, Mr Jones'," George said in a deep voice that was the best impression of God he could manage. "'Therefore, I'm going to give you piles. That'll take the spring out of your step!' And what about those angels eh? What a great bunch of fellas they are! God, it must be just like being a member of the Masons up there. I hope I don't get blackballed when it's my turn!"

"I'm sorry Mr Eldritch. Please ignore my brother. He's got this disease called Idiocy. He's had it since birth, but it seems to be getting worse," Ivor said with irritation.

"This is why people don't like me," Eldritch said, his voice quaking with emotion. "Even when I try to be nice, people find me boring. I can't win. They're either frightened of me or I bore them to death."

"You ought to have a chat with Doctor Stumpf," Ivor suggested. "He's particularly good when it comes to matters of the heart."

"Well, let's let him out then!" Eldritch said, jumping from the bed and pulling open the wardrobe drawer, exposing the semi-clad body of Doctor Stumpf filling the drawer so completely it looked as if he'd been poured in.

"And this time, no tongues," Eldritch warned, as Ronald sat up in the drawer with a suggestive look on his face.

"Ronald, you remember Mr Eldritch," Ivor said.

Ronald squinted at Eldritch.

"Eldritch my arse!" Ronald replied.

"God, his eyesight must be going. It's all that reading he's doing. I bet his palms will be hairy next," Ivor said to George. "Well, we'll be off then," Ivor continued, rising to his feet.

"You sit down there or, so help me God, I'll take that head off your shoulders," Eldritch snarled, jumping to his feet with his mattock at the ready.

"Alright! You were saying?" Ivor asked, quickly sitting back down.

"Yes - why I'm unpopular - it's not that I don't want to be liked, 'cause I do. It's just that I find it hard to let people get close to me."

"Nonsense! We're all in the same room as you now! How much closer do you want to be?" George asked.

"No, I meant emotionally close," Eldritch said, his eyes filling up.

"I used to know a man down the docks like that," Ronald interjected.

"I suppose it's come as bit of a shock to me to realise how unpopular I am," Eldritch said, ignoring Ronald's remark. "I don't know where it all went wrong. I wasn't like this when I was younger. Alright, so I had the odd scrape - like when I loosened that bell in the church tower and killed the congregation - but what child doesn't get up to the odd bit of mischief? There was no real devilment in me, even when I blew up that vicarage."

"You mustn't be so hard on yourself," George said. "You know, we only get one life and if we're always looking backwards, then we're not living for today."

"That's very good, George. Did you think of that all by yourself?" Ivor asked, looking at George in astonishment.

"Well, no. Old Jones said it to me. He kept looking backwards and kept walking into things. It was only when he looked in front of him that it stopped."

"The things you see when you haven't got your gun with you," Ivor said in disgust, turning back to Eldritch with a real look of fake concern on his face.

"Have you always had this trouble with letting people see the real you?" Ivor asked.

"Definitely. I often go out in a mask," Eldritch said affirmatively.

"We all wear different masks, Mr Eldritch, depending on who we're with," Ivor said sympathetically.

"Oh, are you wanted by the law as well then?" Eldritch replied with surprise. "Yes, sometimes I go out in my Cyrano de Bergerac mask. That's very popular with the ladies as they like the nose," he added. "Know what I mean!" he said, laughing lecherously. "Then again, sometimes I go out in my Shakespeare mask. But I'm not so keen on that. After all, no one likes a slaphead, do they? I also get sick of all these kids coming up and kicking me, then saying things like 'we liked English until we had to sit through your crap, you abstruse swine'."

"Yes. Perhaps we ought to leave the idea of masks behind," Ivor said. "Tell me about your parents instead."

"Oh, don't mention them! I think I told you about my mother. A big fat thing with a moustache like a bush," Eldritch began, Ronald sitting up and taking notice at the first mention of hairy women. "Then there was the old man! He was a skinny little runt with a drink problem."

"Yes, but did you ever feel real affection from them? How many times can you remember one of them taking you in their arms and telling you that they loved you? Did you ever feel wanted?" Ivor delved.

"Balls! My parents never told me they loved me! The only affection I got was when my father hit me with an unbroken bottle instead of a broken one," Ronald interrupted. "He didn't need to say a thing on those days for me to see the love in his eyes. And as for feeling wanted? Of course, I was wanted! There was even a reward out for me when I was younger!"

"Bottles? Sounds like luxury to me!" Ronald said, folding his arms in superiority. "Mine hated me and I tell you another thing! It's never done me any harm! They were really great - unbelievable. *Nobody* knows more about parents than me ... tremendous people. And look at how really great I've turned out!" he added, looking around the room for admiring glances. "People come up to me all the time and ask me 'How did you turn out

so great?' and I tell them it's just the way I am …
tremendous!"

"Lying git, his father was a millionaire and he
was a spoilt brat," Ivor whispered to George. "Well,
I think it depends on how sensitive the child is," Ivor
said to Ronald. "Ronald, you were a well-adjusted
and robust child and, therefore, have become a well-
adjusted and robust adult. Maybe Mr Eldritch had
sensitive leanings."

"I told you. Just like that bloke down the docks.
He used to lean sensitively for a penny a go … uh, so
I'm told," Ronald said, looking around the room
furtively.

"No, to tell you the truth, Mallard, I never really
felt wanted. The only time I was held as a child was
when they were checking how heavy I was, to see if
it were me or the turkey that was going to be the
next Christmas dinner!" Eldritch said, casting
Stumpf a sidelong glance.

"Ahh, now that's good! If you can cry at
something like that, it shows you can feel something
inside. How do you feel when you see a couple in
love? Does it make you cry for the little boy inside
you that wishes he were in love as well?" Ivor
probed.

"Little boy inside you? You're not pregnant, are
you?" Ronald asked.

"Ronald! Haven't you ever felt as if there were someone inside you for whom you grieve?" asked Ivor

"Nope. I ate those sausages you bought a few weeks ago and grieved that I'd sold Crusty Jones to the Butcher. By that time there were bits of him inside me and giving me bloody food poisoning! I suppose I do hear these voices now and again, telling me to persecute someone. So, I do, and that's the end of it. I don't like it when I hear them laughing at me and telling me I'm a terrible Doctor."

"No, I can't say as I cry. If I see a couple in love I usually just go and give the bloke a few slaps, tell the woman she could have had me, and that's the end of it," said Eldritch.

"I think we're getting away from the point here," Ivor said, shifting uncomfortably on the bare boards upon which Eldritch had made him sit. "I'd like to know why you think violence is a means to an end."

"Now you really are talking balls!" Ronald protested. "Violence is not a means to an end, indeed! It doesn't have to be! It's enjoyable for its own sake, so long as the person you're hitting can't hit you back! Why hate yourself when you can hate someone else! There's always someone worse off than you so hate them!"

"I know what they say about violence being a form of expression used by the inarticulate man

252

when he feels threatened, but I think that's cobblers! I just like a good punch-up," Eldritch said, nodding in agreement with Ronald, the two of them looking at Ivor for his side of the argument.

"But wouldn't it be better if we could all get along? Why is it so bad to love one's brother?" asked Ivor

"You *sure* you never met that bloke down the docks?" Ronald asked.

"Hang on! We're brothers," George piped. "I'm notloving you, you dirty sod. Anyway, it's illegal, isn't it?"

"Not that sort of loving! I meant just embracing a fellow man and saying 'I love you'," Ivor said with some annoyance.

"Really!" Ronald smirked. Suddenly, there was a knock at the door.

"Who's that?" Eldritch mouthed.

"I'm guessing it's Lindsey … the new lodger," Ivor replied.

Eldritch clambered from the bed and moved stealthily to the door. As fast as he could, he snatched the door open and grabbed hold of Lindsey, pulling him into the room and sending him crashing to the floor.

"You! I know you. You're that bloke I met the other night. You're a bit handy with your fists, aren't you?" Eldritch said, pointing at Lindsey from behind the safety of his mattock.

"Well, I don't like to boast, but it has been commented that I have quite a deft touch. It's only come after years of practice, I assure you. Still, I can't say I recognise your face. Then again, I don't suppose I would, would I?" Lindsey said, dusting himself down before squeezing in between Ivor and George.

"We were just asking whether it's wrong to embrace a fellow man and say 'I love you', Lindsey. What's your opinion?" Ivor asked.

"What is this? Truth or Dare? Of course, I'm all for it, but that's my biggest downfall - I give too much too quickly then, before I know it, I'm nursing a broken heart and they're off," Lindsey said wistfully.

"Right, there you are then. Can we go now?" George asked.

"You stay there! I'm just getting into this! I love the control I have over you all," Eldritch said, his face breaking into a sinister smile as his fingers ran up and down his mattock.

"Yes, you have a problem with power and control, don't you?" asked Ivor. "Was it because you felt powerless as a child, unable to control your environment or the circumstances in which you found yourself? Do you think that's why you seek to control everything around you now?"

"Nah, I just like being horrible and watching you maggots squirm," Eldritch said. "You trying to say to me Genghis Khan ruled his empire with ruthless cruelty, from the Black Sea to the Pacific, just because his mother didn't tuck him in at nights? No! Don't you like looking at the tear-stained face of an old friend as you wrench their teeth out to sell to some backstreet dentist?"

"I do!" Ronald said. "Do you know, gorgeous, I didn't realise you and I had so much in common. I have all this fun causing misery, but you try and tell this pair about it and all they want to do is hug you! Do you know, just yesterday, I was lucky enough to bump into an old friend. As I showed him just how big I am in the britches department these days I could have been right there, back in my old classroom!"

"The happiest days of your life, aren't they!" Eldritch said, going misty-eyed.

"Certainly were. That was the grounding that made me the unbelievable man I am today!"

"Hard but fair," Eldritch said.

"You've hit the nail on the head!" Ronald agreed

"So why are we all up here?" Lindsey asked.

"Because Mr Eldritch is holding us hostage," Ivor explained. "He was in the wardrobe all the time. All that grunting and groaning you heard last night was him."

"Boys! I'm not holding you hostage. I just don't want you to go anywhere so am making you stay here with the threat of violence should you try to leave," Eldritch said.

"Why, though? I don't understand," George asked. "What do you want from us?"

"Well, I must admit, I've enjoyed the probing I've had from the three of you," Eldritch said.

"Ooh, have I missed out on all the fun again!" wailed Lindsey.

"But I'm also waiting for this Uppham character to come with my wad," Eldritch continued, looking at Lindsey suspiciously.

"What do you want from him?" Ivor gulped. Had it all been a trick? Had he, Doctor Ivor Mallard, been duped? Was Sir Richard about to return, having conspired all along with the evil Eldritch? What then?

"Well, I promised to get rid of you lot for him. Good job I didn't, if he had no intention of paying me. Should he turn up today, though, I'll just mug him and let you boys off, seeing as how we're now all friends," Eldritch said, moving to the window and peering down the street, in the hope of seeing Sir Richard.

"Sir Richard? Oh, he's been and gone," said George

"What! When?" Eldritch said, taking George by the scruff of his neck.

"No, he hasn't. Have you been drinking again, George?" Ivor said, panicking.

"No, you remember, Ivor. God, I thought it was me that was thick! A few days ago. That's how we got all the new furniture so quickly, remember? You mugged him of that ten pounds that he had on him ... oops ... sorry, Ivor!" George said, realising too late he'd let the proverbial cat out of the bag.

"Where's the money, Mallard? God help me, I'm not a materialistic man, but I'll kill every one of you if I don't get my hands on that cash!" Eldritch spat.

"It's all gone. We spent it. Like George just said, we bought new furniture and clothes."

"We had all our clothes bought for ... ouch!" George began before Ivor curtailed the latest admission with an elbow to his ribs.

"Hang on a minute! Ronald has got all his left! He only gave us his share for the furniture and I know he's only bought a bullwhip. That man is worth thousands," Ivor said, getting to his feet and pointing an accusatory finger at Stumpf.

"Right then, you old huckster! Business is business and I want some cash!" Eldritch shouted, lifting Ronald over his shoulder and striding to the door with him. "And just in case any of you tossers get the bright idea of trying to escape, I'm locking the door and taking the key with me. If I hear so much as a peep out of any of you, I'll be in here as fast as my fat legs can carry me, ready to kick your arses out of that window."

"Well, I don't think much of him! What a dreadful philistine. Please tell me he's not a friend of yours, Ivor. I simply couldn't bear to go on living here if I thought you fraternised with such people," Lindsey said, as Eldritch closed the door and turned the key in the lock.

"Look, Lindsey, we might not go on living at all. The man is mad! For God's sake, he sold his own brother to a Doctor-cum-resurrectionist!"

"No, he didn't! He sold him to me, actually!" George said proudly.

"Yes, George, I know it was you but I was trying to save you embarrassment."

"But how on earth do you know him? Was he a patient of yours?" Lindsey asked.

"I think I knew his brother first," Ivor said, screwing up his face as he tried to remember.

"Oh, the fat fugger?" George volunteered.

"Yes, the fat fugger. You remember, Lindsey? At the fayre? He was the chap playing Blackbeard whilst his friend danced the hornpipe," Ivor said.

"Oh yes! Do I ever," Lindsey said, a smile on his face as the memory came back to him.

"Yes, well his brother used to get all my medicinal supplies. This was when I was still travelling around from place to place. I think I bought some mummified flesh from Egypt off him and it turned out to be bogus. We took it back and got a refund but the funny thing was that the bogus stuff worked better! When we asked him where he'd got it from, he said his brother made it by painting new bodies in asphalt and leaving them for a few months so that they looked old. He then put us in contact with his brother - Eldritch - and Bob's your uncle," Ivor said.

"And Fanny's your auntie!" George quipped as a shrill scream penetrated the house.

"Oh, God, poor Ronald! What foul perversions is Eldritch exacting on him, just to get him to talk?" Ivor said aloud.

"Perhaps he's showing him some erotic woodcuts of Nurse Conwy," George said.

"Poor Ronald!" Lindsey remarked, wrinkling his nose.

"Yes, alright! Our dear partner is down there now, possibly sacrificing his life so that we might live. I don't think it's right we should be getting some sort of thrill from trying to imagine the most painful death we can think of for him, do you?" Ivor asked.

"Perhaps he's boiling his head in oil!" George said excitedly,

"God, that would be a good one, wouldn't it?" Ivor said, his eyes lighting up. "Or maybe nailing his scrotum to a tree, all the while beating his bare buttocks with a burning log just to make him dance … and dance until he's danced a confession out of him! No, this is not right!" he said, crossing his hands in front of him and throwing them wide apart as though he were banishing such thoughts from his mind.

"We need to do something to take our minds off things!" pondered George.

"I don't think talking about what might be happening to Ronald is going to ease our minds. After all, he might get a taste for torture and wish to refine his craft on us," Lindsey said.

"Oh bollocks! I'd never thought of that," said George, starting to shake, his bottom lip beginning to quiver.

"Look, we must stay calm," Ivor advised, just as a second scream echoed through the house.

"I recognise that scream," George said. "That was the sound old Jones made when I spilt that peppermint oil on his haemorrhoids."

"What a charming story!" Lindsey remarked.

Before any more observations could be made, the sound of a series of banging doors caused the small group to all to hold their breath in terrified expectation. As they listened in mute silence, the sound of heavy footsteps drew nearer and nearer the door.

"Oh, God, we're done for," George said, gripping Ivor's arm and burying his head in his shoulder.

Fancy a Quickie?

"Ronald!" Ivor shouted, jumping to his feet and knocking George into the wall. How did you get out of that? We all thought you were done for!"

"Ivor said he wanted Eldritch to beat your bare buttocks with a burning log and make you dance for him," George said to Ronald as he pointed at Ivor.

"Shut up, George. Don't be silly! Ronald knows I'd never come out with anything as ridiculous as that," Ivor snapped, blushing to the roots of his hair.

"Nobody messed with the Stumpf," Ronald said proudly

"Well? What happened?" Ivor gushed.

"She carried me down to my room and threw me on the bed. She then made a few threats, so I showed her the money and said if she'd like a *Quickie*, the money was all hers," Ronald explained

"Ronald, why are you calling Eldritch 'she'? He's a fat git with a full beard! Anyway, I'm not surprised he didn't fancy a *Quickie*! Those drinks are for *real* men," Ivor laughed.

"Who's talking about the drink?" Ronald slavered.

"You mean ... uh!" George gasped.

"Well, she wasn't having any of it, so when she grabbed the cash there was a bit of unpleasantness," Ronald continued.

"What, you hit her ... I mean *him*?" Ivor asked, his eyes bulging from his head.

"No. I broke wind and she passed out. I dragged her down the stairs and left her on the doorstep," Ronald concluded.

"Ronald, *he* is not a *she*. Put your specs on!" Ivor said in exasperation

"Ivor, I *am* a medical man. I flatter myself I know the difference between a man and a woman. If these chunky babes want to grow a bit of bush on their faces, it's not going to fool me! It just gives us proper men more to hang on to when the real action starts," he drooled.

"Well, at least we're out of that pickle. Hooray for Ronald!" Ivor said, loosening his neckerchief and breathing a sigh of relief.

"Hadn't we better get rid of him off that front doorstep, Ivor?" George asked. "You know, it really isn't good for business to have an unconscious grave-robber on your doorstep."

"Good point. I'm loathe to go and look, but I suppose we're going to have to," Ivor conceded.

As the four descended the stairs, Ivor moved stealthily to the window.

"No, he's gone!" said George cheerily, opening the front door.

"George, I was going to look through the window first," Ivor said. "Supposing he had been there and had jumped on you?"

"Yes, but he wasn't, was he?"

"No, but you didn't know that!" Ivor replied.

"No, but I do now, so what's your point?"

"The point is, be a bit more careful next time and don't be a smart ass. No one likes a smart ass, least of all me," Ivor said, poking George in the eye.

"Is this your dog?" came a shrill agitated voice.

"I'm sorry, did you say something?" Ivor said, looking around the room.

"It was me and I asked you if this is your dog," said a woman, holding Himbry the surgery dog. He panted heavily, little disguising the fact that underneath that bluff demeanour he was looking very pleased with himself.

"Madam," Ivor said haughtily, "You know full well the dog is mine. May I take it that you have some other reason for asking, other than the general enquiry of ownership?"

"He's gone and got my Molly pregnant, that's all," the woman shouted, raising her finger and thrusting it to within an inch of Ivor's face.

"It would seem then, that your daughter should pick her boyfriend's more carefully. Might

263

I suggest a man next time? He's a beautiful dog but he's no ... um ... Doctor Stumpf," Ivor said, getting a thumb's up and a wink from Ronald.

"Don't come that with me! My Molly's my little dog. And your bloody dog has taken her innocence!"

Ivor gasped and took a step backwards.

"Thank you, Mrs Jones. I'll deal with this now," he said, taking Himbry from the woman and closing the door behind him.

The Way the Buggers Bounce

"Oh, God, I don't believe this," Ivor said, flopping into a chair. "Why couldn't you have been more careful? For twelve years I've given you everything! Tried to show you right from wrong, given you a good set of values by which to live and then what happens? You turn around and do something like this! Why, when we were happy as we were, did you have to go and do this? I don't know what your mother would say if she were still alive."

"Now you know why I don't like dogs," Ronald muttered. "No morals. You've brought shame on the house," he added, emphasising his disapproval with a wagging finger. "He's not even taking this seriously! This dog of yours is winking at me!"

"He's not winking at you, Ronald, he's walking away from you," Ivor said in exasperation. "Put on your specs, you vain old fool!"

"I don't need specs! I have the best eyesight. *Nobody* has better eyesight than me!" Ronald said indignantly.

"And what's all this 'my dog' business? He's always 'our' dog until he does something wrong then, all of a sudden, he's 'my dog'. That's just so typical of you!" Ivor retorted, ignoring Doctor Stumpf's boast. "Mymother warned me this is what you'd be like, but would I listen? No! I thought I knew better. 'He's not like all the other Quacks I've met', I said. 'I really think I can trust him', I said. God, I must have been blind to think you were any different from the others! Well, all I can say is that it's not hard to see where this dog has picked up his bad habits, is it?"

"You should write for the fake news! And as for your mother! Don't you start bringing her into this! I was warned at the time that if you want to know what your business partner's going to be like in twenty years all you need to do is look at his mother," Ronald said, waving his arms in despair.

"And what's that supposed to mean?" Ivor said, standing up and moving over to Ronald who had now folded his arms in affected superiority.

"Do I really have to explain?" said Ronald. "I'd have thought that your father would have been the one to tell you - that is if he's still allowed to have an opinion that doesn't differ from your mothers!"

"That's a horrible thing to say! That woman spent hours – literally, *hours* - on my education, turning me into the caring person I am today. I don't think your mother ever did the same, did she?"

"You leave my mother out of this," Ronald said, Ivor's barbs suddenly penetrating Ronald's paper-thin armour.

"Oh, now we've found a weak spot, haven't we?" Ivor said smugly. "The truth hurts, doesn't it!"

"Well, at least my mother was my real mother! My mother didn't give me away because I came a poor second to the Christmas turkey!" Ronald said vehemently.

"How dare you! Get out of my house," Ivor said, taking Ronald by the arm.

"But I've only got my drawers on!" Ronald protested.

"Well, you should have thought of that first, shouldn't you?" Ivor hissed.

"Besides, it's my house," Ronald said, playing his trump card.

"Then get out of *your* house!" Ivor shouted.

"Hold on a minute. Aren't we getting away from what this argument's all about?" Ronald asked.

"Yes. Yes, we are," Ivor agreed. "You see the trouble you've caused?" he added, turning roundly on Himbry, who now hung his head in shame. "We never used to be like this! We were happy until you dragged our good name through the gutter!"

"I don't know what you were thinking," Ronald added solemnly. "Didn't you stop to think of the consequences for just one second, before following such impulses? Weren't you capable of any self-control?"

"Now I see how it really is! You've never cared for us at all, have you?" Ivor said, looking at Himbry who, by now, was lying on the floor with his paws over his face, looking thoroughly ashamed of himself. "We were just a convenience for you. Somewhere to lay your head and fill your stomach while, all along, you led a life of depravity - a life you knew would be the ruin of us! Is that how you repay us? Is it? You don't even seem like the same dog I nursed as a little puppy. You were such a beautiful little puppy," he added, wiping a tear from his eyes. "I was so proud of you that first time you brought your stick back to me. So proud that first time you sat when I asked. I can't help asking myself 'where did it all go wrong?' Was it my fault? Was it something I said or did?"

"I knew naming him Hombre was a mistake! He's a Mexican!" said Ronald, waving a finger at Ivor.

"Come on, you two," George said, in his most sympathetic tones. "You only did what you felt was right, all along. There's no sense in pointing the finger now, trying to find someone to blame. All we can say is that it's happened, so let's deal with it."

"Yes, you're right, George. I know that. It's just come like a bolt from the blue. I'm too young to be a grandfather!" Ivor said, dabbing his eyes. "And I'm too old to hear the scamper of tiny paws about the place. Getting up in the middle of the night, making sure they're clean and fed, worrying myself sick when they're ill. I can't take it! I'm not a young man anymore."

"Are you happy, eh? Happy now that you've caused so much trouble?" Ivor said tearfully, leaning over Himbry, who shuffled uneasily and slapped his lips in self-consciousness, before lying on his side and trying to dig a hole in the carpet in which to bury his shame and humiliation.

As the tension in the room became so heavy it threatened to suffocate the group, there came a defiant knock at the door.

"Oh, balls! If it's that Jones' woman she'll get a piece of my mind, just see if she doesn't," Ivor said, angrily getting to his feet and marching to the window.

"And mine!" added George, helpfully.

"Who is it?" asked Ronald, watching the colour drain from Ivor's face.

"It's Sir Richard. I thought we'd seen the last of him. I knew he wouldn't go to the law on us because they'd ask too many questions but I didn't think he'd have the balls to come back here, especially given that plan of his that Eldritch told us about," Ivor said, suddenly turning into the room and pacing up and down in a frantic, scheming manner.

"Daddy! Ivor said it was you. He saw you through the window," said George who, unseen by Ivor and the others, had opened the door and beckoned his father to enter.

Ivor stared incredulously at George, wishing a huge weight would suddenly fall from the sky and smash him into the ground.

"George. I suppose I don't need to ask if your brother is here as well, given you've already said that he is. May I come in? There's something I feel you both ought to know," Sir Richard said flatly.

"Sir Richard! I hope you didn't take offence at my little joke last time you visited? I'm afraid my humour can be a little black at times," Ivor said, bowing and smiling as broadly as he could manage.

"Joke? Well, I didn't see the funny side," he muttered, making himself comfortable on a sofa. "I hope you don't mind, gentlemen, but the matter is rather delicate," he added, looking at Ronald and Lindsey, neither of whom took the hint to leave the room.

"Well, it's nice to see that you've got all your furniture back. That must have been some joke, moving all that just to kid your mother and I that you'd been burgled," Sir Richard said suspiciously.

"Oh, no, we had been burgled. All this furniture is new," George said. "And do you know, the funny thing is that that desk over there," he added gesturing, to a Dutch oak bombé fronted bureau in the corner of the room, "had letters from you to a man who lived in this house at the same time as me with the same name! Can you believe that? Talk about strange coincidences!" George added, shaking his head in amazement.

Sir Richard looked astonished, then a little confused, before finishing in a state of agitation.

"And that's what you firmly believe, is it?" he asked.

"No. I'm afraid George is entirely mistaken in the matter," Ivor interrupted.

"Well, thank God one of you has a little sense," said Sir Richard, breathing a sigh of relief.

"You idiot, George!" Ivor continued, giving George a slap around the head. "Sometimes you can be such an embarrassment! Those letters weren't in that bureau at all - they were in the desk upstairs! Yes, you wouldn't believe that for a coincidence, would you? When George first showed me, I could hardly believe it myself. I mean, someone with the same name, getting a letter from you, living here and keeping it in a desk just like the one we used to have. I mean, what are the chances of that! I don't know about you but I find the whole thing a bit spooky."

Sir Richard looked from Ivor to George and back again, trying to find some nervous twitch, tick, or trace of a smile that would betray the two as having another joke at his expense. e didn't believe the first one to be a joke and the expressionless faces that now greeted him indicated this was no joke either.

"Well, perhaps I was bit impetuous last time, disinheriting you both," Sir Richard began. "You're my sons, and even if I don't like either of you, I feel duty-bound to let you know where you stand financially. As you might know," he added, before moving to the window and clasping his hands, self-assuredly, behind his back, "I sowed a few wild oats when I was younger. For years, Ivor was under the impression he was a bastard, but I felt he should know he was not."

"Yes, he is!" interrupted Ronald.

"What have I done now?" Ivor asked, his bottom lip beginning to quake.

"Anyway, as I was saying …," Sir Richard said.

"Yep, and I'm rich, baby!" Ivor said, pretending to shoot George with a make-believe pistol.

"That's what I wanted to talk to you about. You *were* rich," Sir Richard began.

"Hold on a minute! What's all this 'were' business? George was the heir until my handsome face popped out of the woodwork. I'm still the oldest, so what's changed?" Ivor asked, his face dropping to the floor.

"Well, I was married before I met your mother. I was always led to believe that my first wife was tragically clubbed to death by a gang of crazed Eskimos who mistook her for a walrus as she took the sea air at Weston. This, I've come to find out, was a mistake. She was not bludgeoned at all but simply left me for a sailor she'd met on a day trip to Frinton. I've recently received communication that she had been with child when she left and that her new man brought the children - I say *children* as I'm told they were a *pair* of strapping boys - up as his own, giving them his name. I've also found out they moved back to this area sometime later, both children going on to be upright pillars of the community."

"Who are they? Do we know these people?" asked Ivor, his mouth going dry as he felt the money slipping through his fingers like grains of sand in an egg timer.

"Not Mrs Jones down at the brothel? I just knew it would be him! I could tell by the way his eyes were too close together, just like Ivor's," George said, shaking his head at yet another coincidence.

"No, George, not a brothel keeper. I'm afraid I don't know the children's given names, only the surname - Eldritch," said Sir Richard.

To Ivor, the words seemed to echo around the room for centuries.

"Oh, no! Please tell me this can't be happening!" Ivor said, resting his head in his hands.

"Yes, well you're not the only fertile one around here!" George taunted Sir Richard, the penny having finally dropped.

"You mean ...?" Sir Richard said, turning from the window.

"Yes! Himbry's going to be a father as well," George said smugly.

"My God, what's that?" Ivor said, suddenly looking up and pointing through the window.

Sir Richard quickly turned, and as he did, Ivor propelled himself from his chair at high speed, pushing Sir Richard from the window so that amidst the shattering of glass and the splintering of timber, he tumbled to the road below.

"Oh, I get it! The old push-your-father-from-the-window-and-into-the-street routine, eh? Very clever," said George, trying another tactic he thought might give the impression of intelligence or foresight.

"No, George, you have no idea why I did that, so don't pretend you do. I was thinking of asking if he'd excuse us, but I knew he'd be too suspicious after what we did to him last time," Ivor explained.

"Oh, that practical joke you played! That was very funny," George laughed.

"No, George, it wasn't a joke. I was lying to make him believe it was a joke," Ivor said with increasing irritation.

"Well, you certainly had me fooled, you cunning old dog you!"

"Look, George, just shut up a minute, for God's sake! I pushed him from the window to buy us some time," Ivor said.

"Oh, has he got some more money on him then?"

"Eh? No, *buy us some time* is a figure of speech, halfwit! God, if I could buy time then I'd buy the last ten minutes back and push you out of the window instead," Ivor said, grabbing hold of George by the scruff of the neck.

"Oh right!" George said, as if the way Ivor had now explained it had fully clarified his misunderstanding.

"Yes, so listen. Sir Richard is lying out in the street unconscious, right? He hasn't changed his will yet, as he's only just found out that Eldritch is his legal heir, follow? Therefore, if we can stop him changing the

275

will, all the money will still come to me ... uh, I mean us. Understand?" Ivor asked.

"Ooh, I don't know about that! If Eldritch is his legal heir, then it should be him that gets the money," George said, pursing his lips, sucking in air and frowning.

"George, you don't understand. It also makes Eldritch our half-brother! It's bad enough that I'm related to you, without having to be related to him and that ridiculous fake pirate brother of his as well," Ivor reasoned.

"Still the law's the law ... ouch!" George began, doubling up in agony as Ivor kneed him in the groin.

"I would explain further, George, but we just don't have the time."

"I thought you said violence was never a means to an end?" George gasped breathlessly.

"It is for everyone else. I'm different," Ivor said, lifting George to his feet.

"Right, this is what we'll do. We'll bring him in. You or Lindsey can give him a *Knee Trembler* - which reminds me, I'll need to get some liniment rub. Make sure Ronald is kept in another room but slip him a couple as well.

"Er, I am still here," Ronald said, his attention having wandered as no one had been talking about him but reanimated at hearing someone mention his name.

"Meanwhile, I'll nip down the shop and get a false beard, stick it on Sir Richard and let the mighty Ronald weave some magic. If those witch-prickers could get those women to recant their witchcraft, it shouldn't be hard to get old Sir Dick to recant the fact that he's Eldritch's father."

"We'll knock some sense into him!" George said.

"That's the spirit!" Ivor smiled, giving George a pat on the back.

"Remember what I've always said, George - cash ..."

"Cash ...?" George queried, frowning and rolling his eyes.

"Yes, George, *cash* ... where does cash come, George?"

"Oh sorry, *cash comes first*!" George shouted, his face breaking into a beaming smile.

"Right then, let's go and get him inside," Ivor said, rubbing his hands.

"Said the spider to the fly," George said, seeing Ivor rub his hands and copying him.

"Eh? Can't you keep your mind on the job? Why are you talking about flies and spiders?" Ivor asked, curling up his top lip and frowning. George nodded a *no*, indicating an explanation wouldn't be worth the effort, so Ivor pressed on, moved to the door and, checking that no one was in the street tip-toed down the steps, closely followed by George.

"Bollocks! He's gone!" Ivor shouted in disbelief, staring at a dent in the road.

"Hey! Keep that language down! It's not hard to see where that dog of yours gets it from," shouted Mrs Jones from next door, slamming the upstairs window from which she was leaning before Ivor had a chance to respond.

"And not hard to see why that dog of yours had to go elsewhere for some affection, is it!" Ivor shouted.

"Doctor! Doctor! Thank God I've caught you!" a local muttered, hobbling up the road and holding his side as blood seeped through his fingers, dripping down his soiled clothing and onto the floor.

"Yes, what is it?" asked George.

"Hang on a minute, I think you'll find he was talking to me," Ivor said, pulling George's arm so that he turned to face him.

"What! I didn't hear him say *Doctor Mallard*, did you?"George asked.

"Well, I'm the more senior Doctor, so he's obviously going to be calling for me, isn't he?" Ivor said, looking George up and down with contempt.

"By 'senior', I suppose you mean old?"

"How dare you! Experience counts for everything in matters like this."

"Maybe. Of course, some would argue that those keeping abreast of the latest developments in medicine are the ones at the forefront of patient treatment."

"Please," said the man. "I don't care which one of you treats me."

"Well that's charming, isn't it?" Ivor said. "I could just be a lump of meat to you, couldn't I, just so long as I satisfy your selfish demands! What do you think I am? Some sort of a surgical slut? You're just the type of man who gets a wife simply to cook and clean for him, never sparing a second thought for her feelings! No wonder she never wants to sleep with you! She could be just *anyone*, couldn't she! You come home after an easy day's begging, expecting your food on the table, then its drawers down for a quick knee-trembler, isn't it! There's no love there! She could be anyone, just so long as she'll let you get on with your filthy business! She's just someone on whom to slake your vile lust! Well, let me tell you, buster, you're not going to use me like that! I'm no medical moll! If I wasn't good enough to begin with, then I'm not good enough now! There now. I've had my say. I don't think there's anything further to discuss between us."

"Actually, Ivor, I think he's stopped listening," George said.

"Typical! These people come along, expect you to drop everything just to treat a gaping wound in their stomach, and what thanks do you get? I'll tell you what thanks you get! None. No bloody thanks whatsoever. Then they can't even be bothered to listen to you!"

"No, I think he intended to listen, it's just that he's slipped into unconsciousness," George said.

"Typical! Just because they can't get their own way, they slip into unconsciousness! Don't fall for it, George. It's only a step up from crying and stamping their feet. Well, I'm not treating him! If he wants to play the martyr then that's entirely up to him. I'm sticking to my principles on this one. My God, whatever next!"

"Hang on, let me check his pockets," George said, bending over the man and rattling a pocket full of coins.

"Money?" said Ronald, his beady eyes ceasing to swivel for a moment. "This is going to be really great – unbelievable. *Nobody* knows more about gore wounds than me … tremendous," Ronald said, having left the house to listen a little better when the commotion started and now trying his best to appear concerned.

"He won't thank you for it. He'll wake up and it'll be 'oh thank you, Doctor,' and he'll trundle off back to his hovel without even asking your name."

"Still, if he's got money then it's the right thing to do," Doctor Stumpf said, dragging the man by his collar to his surgery.

"Ooh, that's a nasty one," George said, having helped place the man on the surgery table and lifting his shirt. "Looks like he's been gored by a bull. Now ..." George continued, looking around the room blankly, evidently debating his next move.

"Cauterise the wound?" Ivor suggested.

"I know," said George wiping his finger on his coat before dipping it in the bloody hole. "Well, it's deeper than my finger, anyway," he added.

"Shall I stick a poker in the fire?" Ivor asked, lighting his clay pipe from a taper he'd lit from the surgery fire.

"Ivor! I'm trying to treat a sick man!" Ronald said.

"I meant a poker to cauterise the wounds not to poke the fire!" Ivor retorted

Ronald nodded a *yes* as he lowered his face to the bleeding hole and peered inside.

"Here, let me have a look," Ivor said, taking the pipe from his mouth and blowing a plume of smoke across the man's stomach, before placing his eye to the hole.

"You always try and take over, don't you?" Ronald protested.

"Just stick your poker in his hole and let's have a think about where Dick's gone," Ivor said, brushing all protestations aside.

"Ooh, I hate doing this," George said, taking the glowing poker from the fire and walking toward the man.

"Then let Ronald do it! He loves doing them! Trouble is, he likes doing them even if there's nothing wrong with the patient."

"Right, here goes," George said, plunging the poker downwards, looking the other way at the last moment.

"George, I hate to tell you this, but you've missed. That's his navel you've just cauterised! Good job the cut wasn't on his buttocks, eh? We'd have another Edward the Second on our hands!" Ivor laughed.

"Oh, it's no good! You'll have to do it," George said, handing Ronald the poker.

"Alright. Let's get this thing hot," Ronald said, walking to the fire and plunging the metal into the hot embers. "I should have been a blacksmith, you know. I'd have been a great blacksmith! *Nobody* knows more about being a blacksmith than me!" he added. Gesturing to the unconscious man with a flippant nod, he took the poker from the fire and walked back to the table. "Right then, here we go," he said, plunging it into the gaping wound. A loud hissing noise erupted as the skin blackened and burned, then curled up like overcooked meat. Skeins of smoke billowed from the burning flesh.

"Oh, God, that smell!" George said, turning away and retching.

"It's lovely! Reminds me of Christmas," Ronald said, sniffing even more than usual.

"Burnt food does not smell like that!" George remonstrated.

"Not the food, you halfwit! When my father came home, realised the food was burnt, and set fire to the cook. The whole family knew he was just being sarcastic," Ronald added.

"Right, we'll leave him here till he comes round," George said.

"Get the money first. You know what these people are like. They see the job done and they run out on you. What can you do then? You can't undo what you've done, can you?"

"You could always stab them," offered George.

"Don't start listening to Ronald about these things. That's the sort of thing he'd do, but no brother of mine is going in the stocks for stabbing his patients. We have the good name of Mallard, Stumpf and Uppham to think of, remember?

"Speaking of Upphams ..." reminded George.

"Yes. I wonder where that little toerag's gone. It comes to something when you can't even throw your own father from a window without him running off. I don't know what's happening to this country. In my younger days, you could throw someone from the roof and you knew by the time you got down they'd have the decency to still be lying there."

"And they say it's all the young people's fault," George said.

"I know! What can you expect when so-called pillars of the community like Sir Richard Uppham are up and away?"

"He hasn't stopped for one minute to think about the example he's setting to us," George said in disgust.

"No, you're quite right. It's alright for him and his generation though. It's us youngsters who'll suffer when we get to their age and find the country ...."

"Like Mexican!" Ronald interrupted.

"Isn't it Mexico?" Ivor queried.

"I know words. I have the best words! Nobody knows words like me," Stumpf blustered.

"Ah, well - imagine that, eh! Anyway, we need to think about this. Already I can feel that huge estate of his slipping through my ... uh, *our* fingers," Ivor said, staring anxiously at the floor as he curled and uncurled his fingers into a clenched fist.

"Well, my money's on Eldritch turning up. Remember when Eldritch was here? He said Sir Richard had promised him money to get rid of us. That means Sir Richard must know who he is," George posited.

"Yes, you're right! I should have known they were related by the way the buggers bounce when you throw them through windows," Ivor said angrily. "So, you reckon he's gone in search of Eldritch, eh?"

"Oh, yes! But who's to say he's hasn't told Eldritch the same story he's told us? Maybe he's playing us off against one another - maybe he's kept Eldritch for all these years with a promise that the estate is going to be his, only to now tell him you're a long-lost son, so all the estate is yours."

"God, that would annoy him, wouldn't it? Still, you might be right. Eldritch was a lot friendlier than usual the other night, wasn't he? And he wanted to talk about family and things ... hang on a minute! Eldritch would never believe I'd been unmasked as his elder brother! I look years younger than he does," Ivor protested.

"I look younger than both of you!" Stumpf said, shrugging his shoulder and closing his eyes as if to indicate that was just the way of things and he had long ago learned to accept that he was far more well-endowed than other men.

"Oh yes, I, uh ... hadn't thought of that," George said, pandering to his brother's vanity. "But what I don't understand is why Sir Richard wants us all out of the way. After all, he helped with an allowance. Now all of a sudden he wants us out of the way."

"That's something I can't answer, George. But I bet I know what's at the heart of it – money! He must have some money-making scheme that we're spoiling. God, it makes me sick that people can put money before their flesh and blood!" Ivor said, shaking his head in disgust.

"But why doesn't he just give us some money to go elsewhere, if all he wants is the house?" George persisted.

"I don't know! I'm not a flippin' philosopher! Why don't you ask him when you see him?" Ivor snapped. "But you could be right about him playing us off against Eldritch. If that's the case, we can certainly expect him to come along sooner or later, just to put a grotesque end to my life of quiet contemplation and healing.

"That said, we know how thick Eldritch is - he might just think 'older than me - oh, it couldn't *possibly* be Ivor, it must be Ronald'. Which gives me a great idea! Obviously, Eldritch is going to be back, right?

Well, we know he's not going to turf us out as he said he wasn't going to the other night, right? If what you think is true, he's going to be told today that I'm not only his brother but the heir to the estate as well, so he's going to come looking for *me*. If we can persuade him the person he wants is Ronald, we're home and dry," Ivor said, breaking into a wide smile and throwing his arms around George.

"Hang on a minute! Supposing he's come here to kill the heir to the estate and we persuade him it's Ronald, doesn't that mean he's going to kill Ronald?" George said with slow suspicion.

"Uh ... no," Ivor said emphatically, not daring to confirm George's insight and realising that Ronald was still in the room.

George's eyes began to roll as he screwed up his face in contemplation, looking towards the ceiling for divine inspiration.

"Oh, yes it does!" he said, after lengthy deliberation.

"Oh, who cares about that old twat! He's had a good innings anyway. He can't grumble, can he? Besides, which would you prefer? Ronald up and about or me ... uh ... us with our hands on that cash? Remember what I said now?" Ivor asked in expectation.

"Cash comes first!" George said proudly.

"Good boy!" Ivor replied, patting him on the head and giving him a sweet from his pocket.

"Listen! What's that noise?" George asked, craning his neck and straining to listen.

"It's someone trying to break in! Oh, God, it must be one of them," Ivor said, beginning to shake.

"Wait here! I'll have a look," said George, moving to the window of his surgery and peering out into the road. "You're right! It's Eldritch. No sign of Sir Richard though. Only Eldritch and that dog of his.

I am Don Juan

"Right then, here's the plan," Ivor said, drawing alongside and leaving Ronald out of earshot. "You go and finish off Eldritch, while I hide."

"Alright. What then?" George said, nodding his head in affirmation.

"That's it. That's the plan," Ivor said.

"But what about the plan we had to give Ronald enough alcohol to boof and let nature take its course?"

"Good! I like that idea. Yes, I'll go and give Ronald a few cocktails and tell him his lady friend has turned up and she can't wait to see him," Ivor said rubbing his hands and congratulating himself on his cunning.

"Right, let's do it!" George said enthusiastically.

As quietly as they could manage, George and Ivor crept from the surgery and back to the living room.

"God, I can hear him! He's out there being unstable, I just know it," Ivor said fearfully.

"It's alright for you! All you have to do is give Ronald a *Knee Trembler*. It's me that has to face *him*," George replied, his teeth beginning to chatter.

Congratulating himself on his plan, Ivor mixed two large jugs of drink, stopping every time he heard a twig snap or a leaf rustled outside.

"Oh, no! I forgot we're out of liniment rub!" Ivor said to himself, looking at the two empty bottles in the drinks cabinet.

"Oh, just use some of that anaesthetic instead," George suggested.

"Yes, he'll like that! Hot and sweet, just like his ladies!" Ivor replied, pouring some diethyl ether into the jugs.

"There should be some morphine over there as well. Give him a good slug of that. That should loosen him up!" George continued.

"By the way, George, have you got anything with which to hit Eldritch?" Ivor asked George who, by now, had moved to the window that afforded a view of the front porch.

"Only these," George said admirably, raising two clenched fists and adopting a sparring stance.

"As I thought! Nothing. Well, just in case Ronald doesn't want to play ball, you'd better come with me," Ivor gestured, nodding to Nurse Conwy's former room.

"Why, what's in there?" George asked.

"Here you are," Ivor said, lifting a floorboard. "Here are some chains, some manacles, shackles, a whip, a mask, some all-purpose restraints. Take your pick," he added, handing them all to George.

"But what's all this doing here?" George asked in astonishment.

"Oh, I ... uh ... advised Nurse Conwy to get it in, just in case an emergency like this ever arose. Lucky, eh?" Ivor replied furtively.

"I should say!" said George, taking them from him. "And what a piece of luck all this leather gear is so sticky! Someone could have a nasty accident if it were all shiny and slippery."

"We *want* someone to have a nasty accident, halfwit! We want someone dead, remember? He's not going to die without meeting a *very* nasty accident, is he?" Ivor asked.

"Oh, right! Leave it to me, Ivor! When have I ever let you down?"

"Oh, God, this just isn't going to work, is it? Why don't I just kill myself and get you to hand me to him on a plate?" Ivor sighed.

"Oh, come on, Ivor! Never despair," George said cheerfully as the noise of a dog yelp came from outside. "God, even his dog sounds murderous."

"Yes, thank you for trying to allay my fears, George! I'm off to see Ronald and give him a *Quickie*," Ivor replied, turning on his heels and running as fast as his jugs would allow. Scaling the stairs two at a time, Ivor quickly arrived at Ronald's room. By now, it was late afternoon, so Ivor knew Ronald would be 'relaxing'.

"Ronald! Ronald! It's me, Ivor. Can I come in?" Ivor asked, only to be greeted by absolute silence.

"Oh, God, please let him be in!" Ivor said to himself, putting his jugs on the floor and twisting Ronald's knob.

As Ivor opened the door, Ronald turned around in his chair to face him, the pipe from an enormous hookah trailing from his mouth.

"Peace, man," Ronald mumbled as he slid back into his chair, a look of absolute bliss spreading across his orange face.

"What do you mean 'peace'? Since when have you ever been into peace, you swine! With Devil's Lettuce as well!" Ivor shouted, putting his jugs on Ronald's desk.

"Hey man, don't spoil my scene. I've got a real good groove going on here!" Ronald muttered.

"No. You don't understand! That big woman who was here a few days ago. The one you left on the doorstep, remember? She's back, and I think she's got love on her mind," Ivor said desperately. "I've brought you a few drinks to get you in the mood."

"No, man, I'm just chillin'. Tell her to come back some other time."

"No, you swine! It's now or never," Ivor said, taking hold of Ronald's head and attempting to empty one of the jugs down his throat. Only then did he spot *Doctor Ronald Stumpf's Patented Enema Kit* lying nearby. "I'm sorry Ronald. I would explain, but you're not really in a position to listen," Ivor added, grabbing hold of the kit and pouring the drink into the bag that was still half-full of soapy water. Taking the pipe, he thrust it down Ronald's throat, giving the bag as hard a squeeze as possible.

Ronald's eyes bulged for a moment before he slid to the floor and underneath the desk. Ivor took a step back fearing the worst. The effect could not have been more dramatic. Suddenly the table rattled violently then, as if propelled from the floor by springs, Ronald jumped to a standing position, foam and slaver drooling from his mouth.

"Ronald?" Ivor asked nervously

"No, I am Don Juan. The greatest lover in all of Mexican!" Ronald answered in a fake Spanish accent.

"Mexico," Ivor said, waving a finger.

"Mexican! I have the best words," Ronald said, clicking his fingers above his head as though they were castanets.

"Don Juan? Well, Donald, there's a chunky babe downstairs with a bushier beard than Sancho Panza. Go to it, tiger!" Ivor said, breathing a sigh of relief as Ronald waddled to the surgery window, only becoming concerned when Ronald stepped from the window and shimmied down the drainpipe, dropping into the garden below. Ivor watched in amazement as Ronald then plucked a rose and placed it between his upper and lower dentures, before unbuttoning his shirt and moving off like a flamenco-dancing Don Juan in search of his Elvire - the unsuspecting Eldritch!

"What's going on? I heard someone gagging and had to come and investigate," said Lindsey.

"It's Eldritch. He's back and he means to kill me. I've just talked Ronald into dealing with it," Ivor explained.

"Oh, how gallant of him! It's just like a chivalric romance," Lindsey said, clasping his hands together and smiling broadly. "We must go and see how he fares," he added, leading Ivor to the door.

"I'm not sure. I really think I ought to keep a low profile on this one," Ivor said.

As if circumstances weren't bad enough, at that moment an almighty crash of thunder exploded in the heavens, followed by the gentle patter of rain.

"Oh, no, that's all I need," Ivor said, curling himself up into a ball and rocking back and forth, burying his face in his hands.

"Oh, go on! You're not frightened of a bang or two, are you? A big strapping Doctor like you?" teased Lindsey.

"No, it's not that. This is the first thunderstorm we've had since you lived here, isn't it?" Ivor said, looking up at Lindsey.

"Yes, but I don't get your point."

"Well, George thinks electricity is going to be the power of the future and every time there's a storm, he runs around on the roof in the nude trying to capture power from a bolt of lightning."

"Does he now! Fancy that!"

"The problem is, I've asked him to help me deal with Eldritch as well, but I know full well he's going to be up on that roof parading around with no thought for anyone but himself," Ivor said helplessly.

"Then we must go and look," Lindsey said, creeping along to George's room. Even before they arrived, Ivor knew his worst fears had been confirmed. George's door was open, as was his window. A powerful wind gusted in, blowing the curtains around and giving the room an eerie and abandoned look.

"Yoo-hoo!" Lindsey shouted, leaning from the window and waving. "No, it's hopeless. He can't hear me. What a shame he's in profile. I've always thought his profile his poorest angle," he added.

"Lindsey, please tell me this isn't happening! I've got a madman trying to kill me and who, even as I speak, is trying to break in. My brother's on the roof in the nude, without a care in the world, and Don Juan down there is flamenco-dancing his way around the garden, trying not to get thorns caught in his false teeth! Could things get any worse?"

"Well, it's not looking great for you, is it?" Lindsey said with resignation. "I still think we should go and have a look for this Eldritch ourselves."

"Wait! I have it. If I give you a *Knee Trembler*, you could lay out old Eldritch for me, just like you did the other night," Ivor said excitedly.

"I beg your pardon? You're taking a few liberties, aren't you? I've heard about landlords like you. Isn't it called *payment in kind*? Well, you can forget it, you sordid little man," Lindsey said.

"No! No! I want you to drink it, and then put those hands of yours to some good use!"

"Right, that is it!" Lindsey said, rising to his feet and storming from the room.

"Oh, God! So, it's just me and old Eldritch! Where is Ronald! Oh, God, if only I wasn't so nice then none of this would have happened! Still, if I am to die, it'll prove the saying that only the good die young," Ivor said to himself.

Suddenly there was a loud crash downstairs, along with the sound of splintering wood. Ivor braced himself and walked slowly to the top of the stairs, descending them one at a time until, finally, he had the barest of vantage points from which to see but not be seen.

As he looked down the passageway, the paunchy figure of Eldritch strode into view.

"Ivor, I need to speak to you. I'm very upset by what you just said to me," Lindsey said curtly, descending the stairs behind him.

"Well ... um ... uh ... Lindsey, this really isn't a good time, you know," Ivor said as quietly as possible.

"When *would* be a good time? I won't be fobbed off you know! I don't know why you think you can take such liberties with me!"

"Lindsey, be quiet! Eldritch is down there with bloody murder on his mind, with the bloody murder victim being me!" Ivor hissed, making frantic motions with his hands.

"No, I won't! There are some things about which you just can't keep quiet, and this is one of them," Lindsey said, dabbing his eyes.

"Where am I? What's going on?" came a strange voice. Ivor turned and squinted. It was the local Ronald had cauterised earlier that day. Now wandering around in a daze, he supported himself by resting his hands against the walls, in so doing leaving a trail of bloody smears behind him.

Ivor watched as Eldritch stopped and listened, given he had heard the same voice as Ivor. His nostrils flared as he moved his head, trying his best to find out from where the sound originated.

As the storm howled and raged outside, a huge gust of wind rattled every window in the house, banging the roof tiles and whistling through the cracks, then blowing open the door that led to the cellar, exposing precipitous stone steps that led down into the darkness.

Ivor screwed up his face and closed his eyes, bringing his hands up and wishing he was somewhere else. Alas, if wishes were horses then beggars would ride, for when he opened them again, yet another character had entered the scene.

Himbry, evidently buoyed by his earlier conquest, had now become a canine Don Juan, striding cockily into the hall, evidently acting upon the glad eye he had for Eldritch's dog.

"Come by, girl," Eldritch said hoarsely, slapping his thigh as his dog moved off. It was too late! Cupid's arrows had been fired and, in an instant, Himbry had begun that at which he had lately proven so adept.

"Hey!" Eldritch shouted, striding over to his dog and trying to part the two of them. As the wind continued blowing ruthlessly through his hair, he and the dogs stood atop the cellar steps.

"Where am I? What's going on?" came a voice in the distance.

Eldritch struggled to pull his dog from the throes of passion but to no avail. Only then, like an avenging angel, did Ivor notice the rapid-fire clicking of castanets and the stamp of a Cuban heel as Ronald came racing up the passageway as fast as his bone spurs would allow.

"I see you are waiting for me, my dear!" Ronald leered in fake Andalusian, the seductive effect considerably diminished by the toilet paper stuck to the sole of his shoe.

For a moment Ivor caught the surprise on Eldritch's face, just before Ronald's thrusting hips caught Eldritch roughly from behind sending him crashing, head first, down the stone steps of the cellar.

"Ah, you little tease!" Ronald shouted, quickly following.

"Where am I? What's going on?" came a voice in the distance.

"Oh, God! Thank you! Thank you!" Ivor shouted, blowing kisses towards the sky then running down the stairs and across the passageway, towards the splintered door.

"George, you selfish swine!" Ivor shouted as soon as he got outside, spying his brother on the roof.

"Where am I? What's going on?" came a voice in the distance, the cauterised local now hopelessly lost in the large old house.

"Eh?" George shouted, cupping his hand to his ear and leaning from the roof.

"And put on some clothes! What'll our patients think!" Ivor shouted.

"I'll tell you what they'll think - they'll think you're all as bad as that dog of yours!" Mrs Jones from next door said, poking Ivor hard in the back.

"Listen, you old bag, why don't you bugger off!" Ivor said, spinning on his heels. "Don't you think I've got enough to worry about! I've got a hairy madman trying to kill me, my senior Doctor thinks he's Don Juan and is trying to seduce a hirsute lunatic in the mistaken belief he's a bearded lady, and my brother's on the roof in the nude! As if that wasn't enough, my lodger's crying because I've unwittingly offended him, a gored patient is getting his filthy hands all over my walls and a stack of cash is slipping through my grasp even as I speak - and all because my father bounced when I threw him from the window!" Ivor shouted, his eyes becoming wild and glazed.

Mrs Jones took a step backwards, picked up her dog and ran back to her house.

"What was that?" George shouted, the rain still beating heavily on the roof tiles and his naked body.

"I said I'm going to wring your scrawny neck when I get hold of you!" Ivor shouted.

"Eh?" George replied. "I can't hear you. Anyway, I don't want to worry you, but ..." he added, pointing a little way up the road.

"Oh my God!" Ivor said, turning quickly, only to see Blackbeard Eldritch walking towards him, his face clouded with murderous intent.

Ivor ran back into the house and desperately began piling furniture against the splintered remains of the door. From the few cracks left unfilled, the one-legged buccaneer could be seen drawing nearer and nearer, like a forest fire in its unstoppable fury.

"Well, that's it. I've had it! One of them was bad enough, but there's no way I'm going to get rid of two," Ivor said aloud, resigning himself to his fate. "Oh, God, I'm not a bad person! Why do so many bad things get sent my way!" he cursed, raising his fist to the sky and shaking it defiantly.

Just when Ivor had given up hope and could swear the *clump-tick, clump-tick* of Eldritch's walk was ringing in his ears, there came a terrible crashing of roof tiles followed by a sickening thud as if a ton of clay had been dropped onto a marble plinth. Cautiously, Ivor opened one eye and pressed it to a crack in the door to look outside.

"Look out, George! He's behind you!" Ivor shouted, now that he could see George had tumbled from the roof and landed slap-bang on top of the approaching villain. "George, watch where he's putting that peg-leg of his! Ooh!" Ivor winced, closing his eyes and looking away. "George, quick! Take it out and hit him with it! Hooray, you did it! You bloody well did it!" he added, tearing the furniture away and running into the road.

"I wouldn't let you down, would I, Ivor?" George said, stepping over the ocean of flesh that separated them.

"That's two down, one to go," Ivor said, taking the naked George by the hand and waltzing with him down the street, despite the rain and the sight of Mrs Jones and her pooch watching from her window.

"Mummy!" George said, abruptly breaking from Ivor's embrace and running up the street to a carriage that had just drawn near.

"Is your father here, George?" Lady Francesca asked, stepping down into the street.

"Not yet, but we are expecting him," George answered tentatively.

"Then would you mind if I came in and waited for him?" she asked, beginning to sob.

The rain continued to cut into the three figures as they quickly made their way back to the house.

"Oh darling, you really should cover yourself up," Lady Francesca said to George, just before her attention was caught by the mountain of flab laid out a few feet from the door.

"Oh, not again!" Ivor said, looking at the body. "I don't know who keeps leaving these here!" He looked up and down the street as though he were expecting to see a small army making a hasty retreat. "After all, we're only Doctors, not miracle workers," he added, looking at Lady Francesca from the corner of his eye. George helped his mother step over the body and held her hand as she took a few steps towards what was left of the front door.

"Oh, no! Don't tell me we've been burgled again!" Ivor said, wringing his hands, as the three of them stared aghast at the remains of the door.

"No, it looks like everything's here," George said, glancing up the empty corridor.

"Where am I? What's going on?" came a voice close by, a moment before the local rounded a far-off corner and entered the passageway. Spying the open door behind George, Ivor and Lady Francesca the local ran, as best he could, past all three before falling headfirst into Blackbeard Eldritch, disappearing from view as the rolls of flab folded around him like soft blankets.

An agitated bark came from the top of the cellar steps as Himbry and his beloved struggled to be free of one another, presaging the entry of the practice's senior Doctor.

"She's not the woman I loved!" Ronald cried as he mounted the cellar steps, and came face to face with Ivor, George and Lady Francesca.

"Who's?" Lady Francesca asked, taking Ronald by the arm, and looking helplessly at Ivor and George.

"The only woman that I, *El Burlador De Sevilla*, ever loved," Ronald said, raising one hand in proud defiance as he stretched the vowels of his words to breaking point, whilst slipping his free hand around Lady Francesca's waist.

"George, go and get some clothes on. I'll try and deal with this," Ivor whispered, pulling George to one side.

"Right," George said, giving Ivor a thumbs-up.

"Lady Francesca ... Mother, this is Ronald," Ivor began. "You'll recognise him from your last visit. Unfortunately, he seems to have ..." Ivor's words trailed off as Ronald took Lady Francesca's hand in his and smothered it in mad kisses. Lady Francesca pulled a face, as though a large slug were sliding over it.

"Psst, Ivor!" George said, calling from the same vantage point on the stairs that Ivor had occupied earlier.

"What is it?" Ivor asked, half-running towards George whilst trying to keep an uneasy eye on Ronald.

"Lindsey's very upset. He just said to me that you don't show him any respect and that you wouldn't have spoken to him like that if he'd been a woman!" George said.

"I didn't mean anything by what I said. He's too sensitive. Now, will you get some clothes on!" Ivor shouted through gritted teeth.

"But if Lindsey was a woman, he wouldn't have a pair of these!" George sniggered, adopting a bow-legged stance and pointing at his wedding tackle.

"Neither will you if you don't get your backside in that bedroom and get dressed," Ivor said.

"Oh! That reminds me! The second thing I meant to tell you!" George said, slapping his forehead with the palm of his hand.

"Oh, no! What have you forgotten now?"

"I went to put on some clothes and who do you think I saw from my window? Yes, it was Sir Richard! I have to say, he didn't look at all happy …."

"You saw Sir Richard? Was he coming here? Why didn't you tell me straight away? I think it's a bit more important than Lindsey's prima donna routine," Ivor shouted.

"No, but Lindsey as a woman!" George giggled.

"Look, George, on your head be it but when Sir Richard finds out you've killed his two eldest sons, I wouldn't like to be in your shoes," Ivor reasoned, trying a different line of attack.

"Both of them? It was only the one and that was a mistake!"

"You swine! You had me believe you did it just for me! You didn't do anything of the sort! It was just luck that you fell on him, and then you only hit him because he started hitting you," Ivor said, trying to grab George by the lapels but, given that George was naked, grabbing a handful of chest hair instead.

"Oh, so you want to fight dirty, do you?" George said, pinching Ivor's nipples.

"Look, this isn't getting us anywhere," Ivor winced.

"You're only saying that 'cause you're losing," George said, giving his hands a half turn, back and forth.

"Swine!" Ivor said, releasing his grip on George's chest hair before taking aim with his finger and releasing one well-aimed flick that caught George in that sensitive spot that only men know about, felling him like an axed tree.

"Ooh," George gasped, releasing his grip as he fell into a quivering mass on the floor.

"Play with fire, sonny, you get your fingers burned," Ivor said, blowing the end of his finger as though it were a pistol.

A door slammed across the landing and Lindsey strode past, carrying a suitcase and weeping.

"You don't think he's off out for a drink, do you? I could so do with one," George said breathlessly.

"No, I don't think The Pig and Ferret will be beckoning tonight, somehow. I wonder where he is going?" Ivor said thoughtfully, walking to the top of the stairs and craning his neck to try and see where Lindsey had disappeared.

"Excuse me, have there been any visitors here over the last few hours?" someone asked. As Ivor squinted, he could see it was Sir Richard, who'd waylaid Lindsey at the front door.

"Well, no one's visited me," Lindsey said. "But then they wouldn't, would they!" he shouted, turning and dropping his suitcase. "After all, I'm just a freak, aren't I? Just a convenience! Who'd visit me because they like me when they can visit me and exploit me?" he wept.

"Yes, the swine! I feel the same way. I paid a couple of friends of mine to come around and throw them out," Sir Richard said to Lindsey, looking around the hall for signs that the deed had been done.

"A-ha! Thought you'd got one over on us, did you? Though we'd believe those Eldritch brothers were our brothers as well? Well, you were wrong! We're just too smart for you! We knew your plan even before you did. Then - to the very last detail! - we knew how to outwit you," Ivor said, swaggering down the stairs, full of bravado, followed by George, who had now dressed.

"I've spent a fortune on you useless pair over the years. As soon as I realised that I'd never get the money back, what else was I to do but get this house off you and sell it?" Sir Richard stormed.

"What! That's just what I'd have expected from you! Putting money before your own flesh and blood! You'd see us homeless just to recoup some money! You disgust me!" Ivor said with contempt.

"I've something to announce!" Lady Francesca said as Ronald carried her from the living room into the hall. "Ronald has asked me to marry him and I've accepted," she giggled. "Just as soon as my husband gives me my divorce."

"Ronald?" Ivor said in astonishment, sitting himself down on the stairs as his knees buckled.

"She could not resist the charms of her Sevilla sweetheart," Ronald explained, kissing the end of Lady Francesca's nose.

"Fran! How could you do this to me?" Sir Richard bleated. "I blame you two for this!" Sir Richard said, pointing a stubby finger at Ivor and George. "The best day's work I ever did was getting rid of you and keeping that turkey! Well, if we're on the subject of confessions, here's one! I've disinherited the pair of you!" he added, turning as fast as he could and punching Ronald squarely in the face. In the commotion that followed, George laid a hand on Ivor's shoulder as the two of them watched the fight's progress.

"Well, look at it like this, Ivor," George laughed. "You aren't any poorer, as it was money you never had. And you haven't so much lost a father, as gained a stable genius!"

"Could everyone listen," Stumpf shouted, bringing his tiny orange finger to his lips. "I've lost the only loves of my life twice today so I'm emigrating to America. There's big money to be made over there for a man like me! It's going to be *unbelievable!*"

Printed in Great Britain
by Amazon

72325979R00184